HERE'S TO SWEET REVENGE

Printed in Australia
Cover design by Shawline Publishing Group Pty Ltd
First Printing: May 2023

Shawline Publishing Group Pty Ltd
www.shawlinepublishing.com.au

Paperback ISBN 978-1-9229-9306-9
Ebook ISBN 978-1-9229-9316-8

Distributed by Shawline Distribution and Lightningsource Global

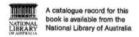 A catalogue record for this book is available from the National Library of Australia

More great Shawline titles can be found by scanning the QR code below.
New titles also available through Books@Home Pty Ltd.
Subscribe today at www.booksathome.com.au or scan the QR code below.

HERE'S TO SWEET REVENGE

B.J. TONIOLO

For Mum & Dad,
Thank-you for a lifetime of opportunities.

To everyone that forms the basis of a character in this book:
Ren, Test, Woofa, Polka, Hughey, Chewie and Westy.
You are all my muses and I am thankful for the years of
wonderful mateship.

To all of those who supported me on my writing and
publishing journey, especially you, Sophie Lewis (#1 fan).

To every member of the crew at Shawline that I had the
privilege of working with, thank-you for helping me to make
my dreams come true.

Prologue

If you ponder the very subject, human life is a bizarre concept really. We are a flash in the pan of existence and largely insignificant in the scheme of things. Despite this, however, we are so full of questions regarding life's meaning altogether, most of which go perpetually unanswered. I think that we search for things like love to give our lives the meaning that we intrinsically desire. And if not love, then things such as wealth, career or adventure are sought to arrest feelings of a meaningless and pointless existence. I know that I did.

I lay here covered in blood, lying on my bed in a silent house. I would once have described my life as perfect, while now I would wholeheartedly say that I'm happy to die. This life can be kind, but it can also be cruel. It can be amazing one moment and then turn on you the next, for no apparent reason and through no fault of your own. Ultimately, I don't think that anyone or anything controls this rudderless ship that we call life. We can control small facets of it but it seems to me that overall, we are powerless to a fate that deals the cards. And sometimes you can be dealt with a truly awful hand. To get to the end, we must go back to the start. Back to when it all meant something. To when life was a wondrous existence that unbeknownst to me, was teetering on a knife's edge, and about to descend into complete and utter chaos. Such is life, that is the expression.

I.

Did you know you can't compare,

The girl with the golden hair.

As beautiful as a flower in full bloom,

A smile that lights up a room.

Chapter 1
Helena

She was still the most beautiful woman that my eyes had ever had the pleasure of viewing. Flawlessly awe-inspiring. Breathtaking. Her hair was a like a warm ray of sunshine. Her smile was the moon and all of the stars in the sky. She was the sun that my planet orbited. She was a dignified grace. A shining light. She was love. She was energy. She was home. The source of my unbridled admiration was my wife, Helena, who stood in the kitchen of our house with her back to the window. She smiled at our baby, Matilda, to reveal a set of impeccably pearly white teeth. I watched them from the kitchen table; the morning light illuminated Helena, putting the delicate features of her porcelain face in slight shadow and making her hair seem even more golden than normal. She was a natural beauty, tall and slender, and one who needed no make-up at all to appear beautiful – the result of an Anglo-Dutch ancestry that had ventured to the great southern land in search of greener pastures in the 1950s and eventually led to her culmination. The love that I had for her and Matilda was almost indescribable.

The first time that I ever met Helena was forever burned into the deepest part of my mind. Although versions of truth deducted from memories can sometimes be clouded by nostalgia and certain details can be shaped by our rose-tinted glasses over time, this was not one of those cases. It was a cold June night, Friday to be exact, when the warm glow of fate decided to shine upon me. I was at a bohemian establishment that was situated in an industrial sector of Melbourne's inner east, as I found myself at the bar ordering some refreshments, ensconced in a familiar sensation of mild intoxication. I had reached a nice sweet spot, one where I could still engage in normal conversation and convey charm and valued opinion if required, but with an altered sense of confidence that I would not normally possess in a state of sobriety – 'Dutch Courage' if you will. There was no audible music playing; only the loud chatter of semi-drunken conversations and general merriment resonated around the room. I stood waiting for my order when I broke from my drunken daze and happened to glance at the person standing next to me. And there she was. Her eyes met my glance as she nodded politely in my direction. She wore a green, knitted jumper with black jeans and hooped earrings that dangled from her delicate ears, dancing with every movement of her head. Her striking blonde hair shimmered as it carved a path halfway down her back. As stated, I was filled with sufficient courage to engage in conversation with inflated self-assurance; something that I would most likely have not done if sober. The opening line was something that always made me cringe.

'I see you got the memo about the green jumpers as well.' I smiled, referring to us both wearing similarly coloured tops.

She returned a look that lit up her soft face, illuminating the most beautiful green eyes that gleamed with the light of the room.

'Yeah, I did,' she replied cheekily. 'Nice to meet someone who follows instruction.'

I was actually quite taken aback by her beauty as my mind scrambled to find a follow-up anecdote. Unfortunately, any further conversation was abruptly halted by the barman who served my requested drinks, which I then paid for and begrudgingly vacated my position at the front of the bar. I wished the gorgeous stranger a pleasant evening before bringing my collection of pint glasses filled with the amber ale back to the table where my thirsty friends waited in anticipation.

'Did you blokes see the bird I was chatting to at the bar? Absolute cracker!'

'Yeah, I did, but I'm that dehydrated from waiting for my beer I thought I was hallucinating. Not used to seeing you chat up good sorts!' my mate Dennis replied in jest.

The remainder of the crew at the table chuckled at his facetious comment and we continued down the path of a more classically blokey chat. The beautiful stranger sat with her friends across the other side of the room and we exchanged fleeting glances with each other throughout the course of my pint. Eventually, the boys finished their drinks and placed them down on the table to signify a conclusion to the evening's proceedings. It was then that I decided that I was not going to be able to forgive myself if I didn't take a chance with the newly acquired apple of my eye. I obtained a serviette from the table and proceeded to write my name and number on it before emptying the contents of my pint with a few nervous gulps. When we all got up to leave, I strode over to the table where she sat. Her distracted eyes locked upon me; nerves began to fizz in my stomach. Before I knew it, I stood at the table with all of its members beholding me curiously. Thankfully, I didn't falter at the realisation of this audience as a gutful of the good stuff had furnished me with a comforting bravado. I took the serviette, which I had folded up in my hand, and handed it to Helena.

'I'm so sorry to interrupt but you dropped this before.'

Her eyes twinkled playfully as she received it and opened it to read. She then looked up at me with a blush-ridden smile; this was the first time that I ever noticed the slight flare of her nostrils whenever she was graced with excitement. I quickly turned and made haste to my friends, who were watching with large smirks on their faces. I had made it about two paces away when I caught my name uttered by the sweetest voice that I had ever heard.

'Jack!'

I turned and looked at its source, who beamed back at me.

'I'm Helena.'

I returned a close-lipped, cheeky grin and nodded, continuing my way in the direction of my friends. I remember hearing the members of her table react with a reprise of giggling, while I was greeted by my mates with a chorus of restrained drunken cheering and back slaps as we exited the venue. I was able to let my adulation become more apparent once we got outside.

'Mate, I can't believe I did that!' I laughed with great satisfaction at my efforts.

Dennis put his arm around me and gave me praise. 'Jacko, ya bloody legend! That was top-notch stuff there. It took guts.'

'Thanks, mate! Now, just gotta hope she actually contacts me!' I said as we made our way into the night.

She did contact me quite soon after that. In fact, it was the very next day that I received a text message from Helena that asked me how my night was and we made plans to see each other the following week. Our first date felt so organic and easy. The conversation flowed so seamlessly and the eventual kiss at the end of the night was equal parts tender and electric. From there our courtship blossomed. If we weren't with each other, we were counting down the minutes until we were. The mundane became riveting. I wanted to be in her presence all the time and I wanted the world to know that she was mine. It seemed as if the caterpillars that had laid dormant in my stomach for 32 years had hatched and took flight whenever I was in her company.

I remember lying next to her one morning, breathing in her scent and thinking excitedly, *I've finally found her.*

I'd had previous relationships before her, of course. Ones where I had willed love, forcing myself to think that it was possible and then waiting intently for those feelings to arrive. But, of course, they didn't, because they can't simply be willed. They can't be forced or coerced. In all honesty, sometimes they can't even be explained. It made me realise that in all of my previous relationships, something was absent. Something intangible. Something intrinsic. Something I wasn't aware I desired. Something that I had wanted my whole life but never knew what it was. And she made me realise those things; she was comprised of everything. Our love developed into the type where I didn't want to engage in sleep because it meant less conscious time with her, but when I slept next to her it invoked the most peaceful version of slumber. And on waking, I was so overjoyed to see Helena next to me; I could've just stared and studied every part of her face and body for hours on end. We were insatiable, the attraction and physical chemistry were unquestionable. Simply put, she was the most beautiful woman in the world and I wanted to be with no one else. We were existing in our own version of bliss.

However, it wasn't without faults or trepidation. We both had walls up, although hers did seem more substantial initially. But once she let me in to her world, there was nowhere else on Earth that I wanted to be. I likened it to the song that we had our first dance to at our wedding. It was Bruce Springsteen's *Secret Garden*, and to me, Helena's heart was a place where *'everything you want, where everything you need, will always stay.'*

I actually hadn't always thought a love like mine was possible. At the time of my life before I met Helena, I had shared a similar viewpoint to most individuals of my vintage. When some people crawl into their thirties and find themselves partnerless, they can begin to become clouded with a degree of scepticism and disheartenment at the reality of finding the love that they are searching for. I was in that cloud, albeit mildly. I wasn't hugely cynical or bitter, as my optimism definitely outweighed my cynicism – I was just realistic about it all.

As time elapsed, I was confronted by the possibility that the hypothetical perfect life partner that I had dreamed of, and thought that I would definitely find one day, was not an inevitably forgone conclusion. I had even started to debate whether I was capable of finding love, speculating whether I was simply adept to being able to formulate those magical feelings for another person. I mean, I had never experienced them, so it was entirely feasible that it wasn't possible for me. However, I did believe that meeting a suitable partner and falling in love was influenced by two intertwined factors: the first one being timing. You both had to be ready for the love and commitment of a relationship to give it the greatest chance of success. I had never been one for tiresome old sayings like 'it will come when you least expect it'. I thought that those were said to people who required hope without truly thinking of the practicality of the saying itself. *So, I had to not expect it for the greatest chance of finding it? If I really wanted it, then was it less chance to come?* That didn't make a lick of sense to me.

The second factor was fear, which in my situation, played a big part. The overall impermanence of love that my experiences had provided me with scared me. *I mean, what were the chances of finding a love that endured my entire existence on this earth?* Love by nature could be quite fleeting for me. In so many past relationships, I thought that I'd discovered love, only to have those initial sparks fade in the blink of an eye. The vulnerability of it all scared me the most; the act of leaving yourself or another open to the torment of heartbreak. The profound fear of giving yourself wholeheartedly and then having it ripped away, only to be left utterly devastated, with a direly hopeless feeling of devastation. This was a frightening possibility that confronted a trepid romantic, and to find a person that made me ignorant of all of these fears was seen as no mean feat. I felt that she would've had to have been truly amazing, in fact, near on perfect. A seamless fit for me. The perfect mix of evergreen love and insatiable lust; profound enough to maintain its evergreen in the fade of youth and death of lustfulness, the journey through middle age and the inevitable dawn of old age. To be resilient enough as to endure a lifetime of ebbs and flows. In reality, I felt that she would've had to have been an out-and-out game changer. And when I found her, she simply was. Undoubtedly.

It took me a couple of months to realise that I'd truly fallen, possibly due to my self-preserving, natural predisposition of not wanting to admit defeat at the hands of love or vulnerability. But true love found a way. It wasn't a romantic gesture that led to this profound moment either; it was quite the contrary. I awoke next to Helena in my old share house after an end-of-lease party that my housemates and I had thrown, with a hangover that indicated that I'd overindulged the night before. As I turned to her, I was greeted with the most beautifully tender smile. Her emerald eyes met mine and we stared so wondrously at one another. The window light at her back gave her a brightly warm luminescence and at that very instant, she truly looked like an angel. That was the moment I realised that I loved her. The moment that I realised there was no one else on the planet for me. I had found her, my soul mate. I could only describe it in words as the fuzziest of feelings in my heart, with my body experiencing a warmly contented glow. I articulated this affinity to her a couple of weeks later when I blurted it out at an airport gate as she left to board for a work trip. She didn't reply but rather just returned a longing smile with a gentle embrace, a courteous way of saying 'thank you'.

Despite this, I wasn't disheartened because somehow I just knew that she felt the same way too. She later clarified that she wasn't ready to declare her love at that moment in time, still quite timorous at the vulnerability that those words entailed. However, a week later she returned the favour as we lay in bed together. And with those three small words, our own little world had been conceived. We'd obtained our own version of perfection; a place where no one could ever maim us because we had each other for fortification.

Our bliss was sustained solidly for a year before I elected to propose. I didn't really have the desire to engage in the traditional down-on-one-knee style phenomenon or undertake any form of grand gesture. Plus, I knew Helena had never coveted that either. So, I decided to do it one evening during a driving trip that we had taken across the United States, as we lay on a mattress in the back of the large van that we had commandeered for the expedition. In the campgrounds of Yosemite National Park, I passed her a note that I had written, which read:

'Ain't got no money to buy you diamonds and pearls,

I would love nothing more than for you to be my girl.

I promise to shower you with hugs and kisses,

I would love nothing more than for you to be my missus.'

She read it and stifled a laugh before looking back at me, as I sat up and turned to her, producing an engagement ring.

'Will you marry me?' I asked a little nervously.

Her eyes opened wide and she obscured her mouth to hide her astonishment as tears ran from her eyes.

'Of course, I will.' She beamed, kissing me with the softest of lips and squeezing me with all of her might.

About twelve months later we were married at a winery in an elegantly simple ceremony; neither of us had wanted a big hassle and Helena had never fantasised of having a colossal wedding like some women tend to. She wore the most stunning white dress without a veil, a nod to her practical yet graceful nature. I will admit that I cried when our eyes met for the first time as she walked down the aisle of the little chapel. I was purely overwhelmed by the happiness and perfection of that moment. Just as I was when Matilda was born a couple of years after that, having been overawed by the immediately unconditional love that had for the tiny creature that I held in my arms. She made me feel complete; my heart radiated with the love that parents constantly describe as one that you will never truly appreciate until you bring another life into this world.

I was jolted from nostalgia to the present moment by a loud cry from Matilda as I left the table to pick her up out of her high chair. I rocked her from side to side and after a few moments, she stopped crying and looked up at me. Matilda appeared to have taken after her mother aesthetically at this stage of her existence and had not inherited any of my dark features. I was grateful for this, given how much I coveted my wife's angelic beauty.

'I love you, you little grub,' I said, planting a kiss on her forehead before placing her back in her high chair.

I returned to the table to collect my plate and then made my way into the kitchen to put it in the dishwasher.

'Alright, my darling, I gotta go and make some money,' I said, turning to Helena and wrapping her in an embrace as we kissed each other.

'I love you,' she whispered.

'I love you too,' I muttered, returning the proclamation tenderly before leaving, slightly unwillingly, for work.

Chapter 2
I Never Told You What I Do for a Living

I left the house and was confronted by the brisk crispness of the wintry day as I unlocked my car and hopped in. A breakfast radio show greeted me with the spritely voices of its deejays, which provided a soft backdrop to the contemplative reflections that were undertaken during my morning commute. I was an architect by trade, a reasonably successful and well-renowned one too. Although, my business was solely immersed in residential projects, which admittedly limited its fiscal success compared to those involved in commercial ventures. However, I was never an individual who desired nor found motivation from wealth or money; I was always a subscriber to life's simpler pleasures. My family and I were by no means affluent, but we were financially contented, and lived in an existence that was fuelled by love and happiness and unbound by most of life's anxieties.

I had declared, quite early in life, that I was going to be an architect. In fact, as a young child, I would sketch pictures of houses for days on end. This progressed to Lego models as my childhood marched forward, and eventually in high school, I took to the computer-automated design side of things. Upon graduating from university, I took the first job that was offered to me, thinking that I had entered into what my naive mind had perceived would be my architectural Valhalla. However, I was mistaken. The work at the big firm in the city that employed me was unrelenting. I worked long hours and was insufficiently compensated by my salary in a company that designed immensely soulless buildings where creativity was stifled under the restraint of the almighty dollar. After a period of time, I began to discover a passion that had resided in me all of my life was gently evaporating with every uninspired building that was churned out with my input. Despite this, I slaved away for a few years, shrouded in the mantra that matters would improve. Unfortunately, many a worthy soul has fallen victim to this notion; lingering in a job in the anticipation of improvement, only to eventually discover that they wasted their working lives being miserable, without having searched for greener pastures and absconded the captors of their career. I decided that I was not going to be one of these unfortunates, realising that the only remedy was not time but rather change. This was when I made the move into residential architecture and vindicated my childhood dreams by taking a job with a small firm. With this move, my passion instantly began to re-ignite.

Around a year or so following this vocational shift, I met George Fullarton. He was a builder, who had chosen my footy club to be the location of his socialising activities. He was a bald, middle-aged man, quite tall and broad-shouldered, hardened by years of manual labour and weathered by eons of working in the sunburnt land without protection from its merciless sun. Initially, I had found him to be quite crass and obnoxious at times, but as I delved deeper into his acquaintanceship, I attained him to be a relatively pleasant individual with a good heart, albeit a little rough around the edges. In my opinion, he was simply the product of a bygone era of manhood, one where certain culturally antiquated taboos and philosophies existed, but their expression was not frowned upon like in today's more politically correct world.

This could get him in hot water at times, although his reasonable charm would usually be a folly for any intense dislike or ill will. Some may have termed him an 'ocker' or a 'bogan' but I believed the general consensus to be that of a loveable larrikin. Over time,

I began to accept his larrikinism and he earnt some endearment from myself. So, following some prolonged coaxing from him, we decided to go into business together. I departed from my job at the little architecture firm and 'New Fullarton Builds' was born; a semi-combination of my surname 'Newton' and his. George was the builder who would coordinate the construction of my designs, while I was the engine room of the business. Essentially, I had full creative control over my own projects and no one to suffocate my creations, which was something that I'd always dreamed of. I was also in command of the financial portion of the business, given George was not exactly blessed with intellectual prowess. He was, however, largely proficient in his chosen vocation and we became highly reputable as a result. We worked amiably together as the business pleasantly hummed along following its commencement and as time transpired, a great working relationship developed, along with a harmonious friendship. A few months before Matilda was born, he insisted that his wife, Elaine, take over the financial operations of our company and informed me that she had completed a bookkeeping course in anticipation of the baby's birth. I found this to be quite a gracious gesture, as in all honesty, I had been slightly vexed by the dilemma of juggling a baby and the controls of the business. At the time, the situation all felt perfectly serendipitous.

That morning, I arrived at the site of one of our projects to meet with George and the carpenter on the job, my good friend Ted Worsopp, in order to discuss some design issues that we were having. It was a brisk morning. Fluffy clouds dominated the winter sky as the morning sun attempted to protrude through their cloak. An audible resonance of magpies warbled in chorus from surrounding gum trees, nestling amongst the clatter of a busy building site that smelt like freshly cut timber. We were at the house of a man by the name of Rocco Falcone, a businessman of the area, and given the appearance of his house, quite a prominent one at that. He was also known to be acquainted with the local underworld as many colourful characters were regularly seen in his company. He was not what I would have described as an affable man in the slightest; in fact, I found him to be extremely unpleasant, arrogant and disrespectful in my dealings with him. We were undertaking a substantial renovation of his uninspiringly banal house, which was a modern and boxy façade that was rendered in a faceless grey. It was quite the private estate, mostly veiled from the public by a high rendered fence and dotted with security cameras that were fixed at certain locations on the front.

'G'day, boys!' I said as I greeted them both situated in the front driveway of the Falcone house. 'How we travelling this morning?'

'Good, mate,' George said as he stood with his arms crossed in a confident, nonchalant kind of manner.

'Not too bad, Jacko. How 'bout you?' asked Ted, a slighter, yet athletically built man, who also stood with his arms crossed; however, given that he was wearing tan shorts with a tool belt and a t-shirt during this frigid morning, I inferred that his posture was more reflective of the temperature than a nonchalance.

'Good as gold, thanks, Teddy,' I replied to his question.

'Bloody freezing this morning. George, the lucky bastard, gets to nick off to Bali tomorrow!' mentioned Ted.

George smiled and lent back with his arms still folded.

'Don't miss me too much, boys! I will be thinkin' of you blokes when I'm havin' a froffy on the beach in the sun and you blokes are stuck here freezing your tits off!'

'Actually, the thought of your pasty rig in budgie smugglers with your pills on display makes me pretty rapt to stay here!' I joked.

'Oh, turn it up! The sheilas in Bali aren't gonna know what's hit 'em,' returned George irreverently with a smirk.

'You know he's getting his chompers polished over there!' Ted announced as he turned to me with a cheeky grin and pointed to George's teeth.

I turned and looked mischievously in George's direction as he grabbed Ted by the scruff of the neck in a playful manner.

'Oi! I told you that in confidence, you little wanker!' he responded through facetiously gritted teeth before releasing his grip on Ted and turning to me with a more earnest look and tone. 'I'm not gonna get it done but I did look into it. Years on the darts and drinkin' coffee have ruined my teeth. They charge you like a wounded bull here so I was thinkin' of getting it done there but decided not to. I'll just be getting pissed and sunburnt instead.'

'Don't worry, mate,' I added. 'You already look like a million bucks, anyway!'

Just as we chuckled in unison, the garage door opened to reveal an expensive, dark-coloured sports car that still managed to gleam in the gloomy light of the overcast morning. We all relocated from the driveway to the front lawn to make way for the vehicle, waving as it left the garage. The occupant of the vehicle was Rocco Falcone himself, a cleanly shaven man, quite fit and healthy for his years. He had his dark hair slicked back neatly and wore dark sunglasses, appearing to be dressed in an expensive suit and shirt, devoid of a tie. Despite our pleasant greeting, he stared straight ahead as he drove past, ignoring our gestures and speeding off down the street with an obnoxiously loud, metallic grunt of his engine. His indignant manner only further consolidated my previous opinion of him and seemed to irk the other two just as much.

'That bloke is a fair dinkum cock head!' exclaimed George.

We all laughed in agreeance.

'Getting even a smile from the bastard is as rare as bloody hen's teeth, I tell ya,' Ted added.

'I tell you what, it's been real hard yakka dealing with him hasn't it, Georgey?' I chuckled.

'Bloody oath it has!' George concurred.

'But I s'pose he is paying us an absolute packet to do this reno on his joint, so we need to play nice for the meantime, unfortunately,' I informed.

'Look, I'll take the wog's cash but I've been that close to chinning him a few times when he's spoken to me the way he has. Such a dead set knob!' exclaimed George.

'Oh, mate, me too, believe you me,' I sympathised. 'The bloke seems mad as a cut snake, to be honest. I just wanna get this job done and move on!'

'Too bloody right, Jacko,' replied George. 'Now, let's go over the few questions I have with your plans so we can finish the bastard as soon as bloody possible!'

'Georgey, while I remember,' interrupted Ted. 'You got that cheque for me?'

'Oh yeah, mate. Here you go,' George said as he produced a folded cheque from the pocket of his jeans and handed it to him.

'Beauty! Thanks, mate,' expressed Ted as we started into the work site to discuss the issues that the two tradies were having with the renovation.

I stayed on site with Ted and George until mid-morning before making my way back to the office of New Fullarton Builds. The business inhabited a cosy, newly-built office space that George had acquired relatively inexpensively, due to the fact that he had built it and the landlord had struggled to secure anyone to lease it for a long time after it had been constructed. The idea of having an office had been floated by George from the business's inception but I had initially provided resistance in an attempt to keep expenditures minimal.

However, as working from home soon became quite the distraction with Matilda's arrival, I relented. I parked at the rear of the building and made my way into the office via the back door. From this entrance, you were met by a small kitchenette and meals area, and another doorway, which opened onto a long hallway that ran down the entire length of the workplace. The first stop along this hallway was my office, which contained a small window, a desk and various pictures and photos that I had used to decorate the blandly white walls that I had been presented with when we had begun our tenure.

I stopped to place the items that I had transported from the car on my desk before making my way further down the hallway to the front room to greet Elaine. Her usual domicile of production was a spacious reception area that consisted of a large desk and sign on the back wall, which stated the business name and welcomed an entrant from the front door. The shopfront had a large glass window that faced a prominent main road and could provide adequate distraction whenever one felt cognitions of procrastination.

'Good morning!' I greeted as I entered the room from the hallway to view Elaine seated at her desk.

'Morning, Jack!' she replied as she turned from her computer screen to receive me warmly.

She was a skinny woman in her mid-50s, whose face had begun to show the detriments of her age and life's vices. Her skin was weathered from years of abuse from the sun and cigarette smoke, while her voice was quite raspy, given her years at the mercy of her nicotine addiction. At one point in her life, her short and curly hair was probably a shimmering blonde; however, over time it had been transformed into a lifelessly dull, mousy-grey mass. She was a satisfyingly friendly lady, albeit rough around the edges like George, but I enjoyed her company and furnished her with the same endearment that I beheld him in.

'Excited about tomorrow?' I asked as I stood by her desk.

'So bloody excited, Jack! Don't miss me too much!' She laughed in her dry, cackling laugh that ended with a small cough and a clearing of the throat.

'I'm heartbroken already,' I countered playfully.

'Did you sort out everything that you needed to with George?' she then quizzed after a slight pause and regaining of vocal composure.

'Yep, all sorted now. I've just gotta fix a few little things and make a few adjustments so I'll be in my office if you need me, okay?'

'No worries. Do you need a coffee or anything?'

I contemplated for a second.

'Oh yes, please, that would be brilliant.'

'Righto, give me two secs.' She turned her head back to the computer screen and began typing away feverishly.

I then made my way back down the hallway and into my office to commence the long and tedious readjustments of the extension plans that would occupy my day.

Chapter 3
The Hurry and the Harm

Ted's call startled me from the fixation I had over the screen of my computer.

'Jacko, you'd better get down here. Things are a chance to kick off between Rocco and Georgey, could be on for young and old,' he said worriedly.

I scrambled for my keys and yelled a brief message down the corridor to Elaine as I left before scurrying to my car. The engine sang along with the radio as I took off for the short journey to site. Triple M played Foo Fighters into Paul Kelly, which was followed by the deejay amusing himself with his own voice. I weaved through the streets, thinking about things on the way over. George and Rocco were certainly alpha personalities, but George was always cordial with him, so I wondered what had gone awry between them. As I pulled up, I peered through my car's window to view the scene: Rocco and George were stood on the driveway, yelling in each other's faces, with gobsmacked tradies crowded around them. Ted stood in the middle of the two, attempting to nullify the warring parties as best he could. I jogged over quickly to assist in placation.

'Boys, boys, come on. Ease up!' I pleaded. 'Let's all calm down, we can sort this out.'

I couldn't hear the words that were being said but their voices were sharp and gruff, and cut the terse atmosphere. I grabbed George and pulled him away to the beginning of the driveway;

his tense body was heavy to move and his eyes wouldn't meet mine.

'Georgey,' I begged, staring up at him. 'Please calm down, mate. We don't need this.'

He broke his angered trance with a heavy sigh. 'I'm sorry, Jacko. So sorry, mate.'

I turned to Ted who had come to stand beside us. 'Mate, can you stay here with George while I have a chat to Rocco?'

Ted nodded. I patted George on the shoulder and made my way back up the driveway. Rocco's grey eyes beheld me with abhorrence.

'Can we chat inside, Rocco?'

He grunted, turning his back on me and walking in through the house's grand entrance doors in a huff. I trailed apprehensively, my eyes focused on the marble tiles of the entranceway in avoidance of the vitriolic figure that led me to his study. The stylish curtains of the room's large front window were drawn to veil the precious homeowner from the tradesmen that infested the front yard of his house. A series of bright downlights shone down upon a dark wooden desk that formed the centrepiece, messily decorated with paper documents amid picture frames and a cigar box. The room's beige walls were adorned with articles of sporting memorabilia; a photo of Muhammad Ali was erected on one side, his signature beaming in gold marker. Another wall showed the players of a victorious 1995 Carlton Football Club, grouped together jubilantly with premiership medals hugging their necks. I sat in a chair across from him. The room smelled of wooden leather, with a hint of cigar smoke.

'The Blues,' I said nervously. 'Good year for you blokes in '95.'

He looked at me, his austere face unmoved. 'Don't get me started on that piss weak footy club.'

A tense silence formed around me as I waited for him to re-join the dialogue between us.

'Now, when the fuck is this reno gonna be done, Jack? I'm sick of having all these bloody tradies here. It's a friggen nightmare! I have no kitchen or dunny downstairs. All I have is this office and upstairs. I can't eat here and my missus and kids have left and are staying at a bloody hotel in the city. Not to mention that I gave you blokes extra cash to be done with the renovation as soon as possible. I mean, what the fuck was the point of that?'

I paused for a moment, nodding a little to consider his words and formulate a measured response to avoid inflaming the situation.

'Rocco, I'm sorry for the disruptions to your home life. I know going through renovations isn't the easiest of things to deal with.'

'Got that bloody right!'

'I'll have a chat to George and see if we can hurry things up a bit. We are definitely on track to be done in the time we quoted you at the start.'

'It's not bloody good enough. I paid for you blokes to hurry the fuck up!'

Again, I rested before responding.

'I understand, mate. I'm sorry if you thought things would be different, but we are trying to be as quick as possible and give you the best result. Unfortunately, disruptions happen along the way. But once we're done, I guarantee you'll be happy. I'm sorry if there has been any misunderstanding in the process.'

'Don't friggen condescend me! Your mate out there got on to me for more money and said he'd do things quicker. I gave the fuckwit a hundred grand cash! Stop playing dumb. I didn't get to where I am today by being naive, alright?'

His comment baffled me. I looked into his grey eyes; they were darkening egregiously, like impending storm clouds.

'I wasn't aware of that,' I said timidly.

His eyes blackened; lightning cracked in their cloudiness. His lips tensed ominously.

'Don't fucking lie to me! Get the fuck out of my house and tell all your tradie mates to hurry up and get this shit done! Things will get worse before they get better if you keep testing my patience!'

He slammed his fist on the desk, the sound cracking loudly like a whip. He then stood from his chair and abruptly gestured for me to leave. I bid him adieu with a nod before promptly exiting the house. The air felt lighter outside, cooler on the skin. I breathed a sigh of relief, struck with a serenity after the vicious tirade inside. All of the tradesmen stood stationary by their cluster of utes and watched me walk towards them.

'Strewth, Jacko! You in one piece, mate?' Ted remarked.

'Crikey, reasoning with him went down like a lead balloon! Did you blokes all hear that?' I said wryly.

'Mate, the whole street did, I reckon,' Ted replied.

I looked at George. He appeared more docile. He was almost embarrassed in my presence, like a dog who knew they had done something disobedient.

'Georgey, can I steal you for a few seconds, mate?' I asked.

He nodded timidly. We began to walk down the street, not speaking until we were out of earshot of the group. George broke the silence first, turning to his head look at me contritely. His face was a tired grey, displaying more scraggly wrinkles than I recalled him to have.

'Jacko, I'm sorry, mate. But that bloke is an absolute handful! He just started going off his chops at me for no reason! I couldn't take it, so I bit back. I mean, me and the boys have been going like the clappers to get this job done and he has a go at me for taking too long and disrupting his home. What the bloody hell did he expect?'

'Georgey, it's okay, mate. I know what he's like – he's the biggest tosser I've ever met. At times, I really regret agreeing to do this reno. We should've just said we had too much work on.'

'I just keep reminding myself how much exposure the business will get when we're done. His missus has already organised a TV crew to come out and the Herald Sun to do a write up.'

'You beauty. Well, we need to keep our heads then, even if he's being a bit aggro, okay? We don't want things going from chockies to boiled lollies here, you know?'

'Yes, Jacko. I know, mate.'

'There was one thing he said to me, though.'

'What did he say?'

'That you hit him up for more cash and he gave you a hundred grand to get things done ASAP. That's why he's filthy, reckons you stitched him up.'

He hesitated before responding, his face screwed slightly. 'He's lying through his teeth, Jacko. Honestly, the bloke's off his head!'

'Well, what does he mean exactly?'

He dithered again, appearing a little sheepish before replying. 'I didn't hit him up at all. He came to me when we started at this joint and said that he would give me cash upfront if we hurried things along. Said his missus couldn't stand the intrusion. I didn't want to insult him or make him angry, so I took it. We were a bit low on cash flow for the business, so it was hard to say no to. But it's not extra cash at all – it's just part of his payment upfront and I told him I'll take it off the bill. He must've misunderstood, I dunno.'

'Why didn't you tell me?'

'You've got enough on your plate. Plus, I didn't want you to think I was doing anything dodgy.'

'So, it's all above board?'

'Of course, Jacko. She's all ridgy didge, mate. Elaine is a stickler for all that stuff. She couldn't lie straight in bed, that bloody woman. You can ask her when you go back to the office. Basically, we had those few clients who took ages to pay and then heaps of bills came in. It was perfect timing, really. Elaine would've killed me if I didn't take it and we had to wait a month or so for the money to be paid.'

'The business is financial, right?'

'Oh, yeah, everything is fine. You know how it can get. Our expenses can be monstrous and sometimes you have to wait for money to come in. But once we get this job done and get the exposure, we'll be laughin' all the way to the bank. I reckon any financial stress will be over. We are going places, my boy.'

He put his broad arm over my shoulder and pulled me into him. I instantly felt at ease; his squeeze was laced with comfort and it put to bed any worries that dwelled in my mind. I was well aware of the peaks and trough of the financial side of the business – things like this could happen. When I had kept the books, I'd had a few instances where situations were very similar. I'd even stressed about bankruptcy a few times. There was no doubt that I could trust George and Elaine, especially when compared to the maniacal mafioso that was Rocco Falcone.

I returned home in the evening, just as the sun was setting, and parked my car out the front of our modest weatherboard home. As I vacated the car, I stopped to admire the house in the sepia tone that the sunset had provided amongst a gentle breeze. 43 Harvist St was an absolute beauty: an old-fashioned, double-fronted cottage, painted in a cream and light blue arrangement. Its original blue wooden door stood at the centre, bordered by two double-panelled windows either side of it. A slightly decaying, yet functional, veranda was attached to the front, consisting of posts adorned with decoratively charming wooden latticework. Its picketed fence stood at the front, revealing a paved path to guide an entrant and small patches of grass and shrubbery either side. A large and shady gumnut tree stood on the adjacent nature strip, which maximised the Australiana charm that I cherished and provided a sprinkling of gumnuts to the footpath and front lawn.

We had bought the house with the intention of renovating a few years back, but unfortunately, while the inside had received some affection, the outside had not been mutually serviced. I wholeheartedly adored this house, not only because of the individuals that it housed or the life that it represented, but I also esteemed the character that it furnished the streetscape with. It was a piece of history in inner-city suburbia and a relic of the past before the age of gentrification. My admiration was broken when I heard a rustling coming from the next-door neighbour's house. I turned in the direction of the clatter to view its source. It was our quirky neighbour Bruce, who was noisily pottering around on his cluttered front porch. In fact, the entire front of his house was littered with an appallingly clumsy array of items as a result of his hording. The few times that I had been allowed inside of his house, I had found it quite confronting that a man could happily live his life in the manner that he did. It had been piled so high with swarms of junk that it had been quite difficult to make a clear passage anywhere throughout the dwelling. Bruce spotted me standing on the footpath, stopped what he was doing and moved towards the front fence of his house. His gait was clunky and strained, without appearing to provide any twinge of nuisance to its perpetrator. Once he reached the fence, he leant on it, which indicated to me that he wanted to have a bit of a yarn; an exercise that never consisted of any questions in my direction but rather with me nodding in agreement while he unloaded a political rant or an inappropriate joke that he had heard. Although I found it mildly irritating at times, I knew that he barely entertained any visitors, so I saw it as an obligation of mine to provide him with one of his only forms of social interaction for the day. And after all, it only took a diminutive amount of time out of my life to provide him with a sympathetic ear.

'G'day, Bruce.' I moved over to the fence to greet him. 'How you going, mate?'

'Oh yeah, pretty good,' he replied in his slightly high-pitched, antiquated voice. 'You see what those clowns at the government are doing?'

'Oh no, what?' I asked, feigning surprise and interest at his question.

I studied him in the fading evening light as he began his ramble, his mouth whistling whenever he pronounced 's' sounds. His wilted face was old and wrinkly, dotted with a multitude of white whiskers that he had obviously missed whilst shaving. His white-coloured hair appeared slovenly under his beanie, while his eyes squinted as he talked. Evidently equipped for the cold weather, he wore a couple of sullied jumpers under stained overalls and his characteristic bulky slipper-like shoes, which I believed to be some form of diabetic footwear. I tuned back in as he completed his ramble.

'They're all bloody crooks, I tell ya,' he summarised in a conclusion about his disdain for the people in parliament.

'Yeah, it's a mug's game, isn't it?' I concurred before promptly changing the subject in an attempt to conclude our interaction. 'You got any jokes for me today, Bruce?'

He paused for a brief instant and then simpered mischievously.

'Yeah, I got one.'

'Okay, let's hear it.'

He shifted for a second or two, like a comic on stage in a comedy club who was preparing to dazzle an audience with a clever set-up for a gag.

'Two nuns are riding their bikes in Rome and they head down a street with cobblestones. One says, "I've never come this way before". The other says, "it must be the cobblestones!"'

He started to titter in the wheezy, halting manner in which he usually laughed, while I reciprocated with a polite chuckle. It was actually quite a funny joke, but as is de rigueur, I was always prepared to courteously laugh at his jokes regardless of their comedic value.

'Oh, good work! One of your better ones, I reckon. Anyway, I better get inside, take care of yourself, mate,' I remarked as I turned to go into the house, leaving him there chortling away at his own hilarity.

I entered the house and walked down the hallway to discover the picture of my two beautiful girls in the lounge room, coupled with the wonderful fragrance of dinner. Matilda was on her playmat, playing with her toys and exuding all variants of excited noises, while Helena sat on our couch, watching her lovingly as the television whirred in the background.

'Daddy's home!' I announced as I entered the room excitedly to the favourite part of my day.

Helena smiled gleefully and uttered a greeting, as I kissed her longingly on her soft lips.

'Hello, little grub!' I beamed as I bent down to pick up Matilda.

She cooed as I held her lovingly and swirled about the lounge room.

'How was your day, babe? How's your mate Rocco?' Helena enquired facetiously as she left the couch and moved into the kitchen to check on the meal that she was preparing.

I gave a wry smile and turned to her whilst holding Matilda.

'Well, get this. Firstly, we were standing in his driveway in the morning and moved to the side as he drove out of his garage to leave. We waved at him but he stared straight ahead like he had blinkers on and drove off. Completely ignored us! Then, the icing on the cake, I had to go there in the arvo to break up him and George almost punching on!'

'Oh, gosh! What were they fighting about?'

'Rocco is angry that things are taking too long and there's tradies in his house disrupting everything. Can you believe that? I had to go inside and talk to him. He gave me the biggest spray. Almost tore the paint off the walls!'

Helena shook her head and laughed.

'Yep, he's a strange one alright,' she added diplomatically. 'What did he actually expect?'

'Who knows. I'll never understand people like him. How was your day, anyway?' I said, placing Matilda back on the floor and making my way into the kitchen.

'Pretty good actually. She's been a bloody legend today so I've had plenty of time for all this,' Helena stated as she attended to the finishing touches of the meal. 'It's pretty much done.'

'Smells amazing!' I said as I moved behind to embrace her and kiss her neck.

She stopped what she was doing to savour the moment as I drew her in. She smelt like she always did; it was like a mild sandalwood on a gentle summer breeze. It was a smell of warmth and love. A smell of home.

II.

It's a love,

one in which no one can deny.

An intangible that words fail,

yet always seem to try.

In the darkness of this world,

it is an everlasting light.

In the chaos it is a calm,

that forever shines so bright.

Chapter 4
Your Heart Is an Empty Room

That night my best friend, Dennis Bishop, and his wife, Claire, came over to have dinner with us. Dennis and I were more like brothers than mates, having been friends since childhood and sharing the mutual honour of being best men at each other's weddings. He had been present at mine and Helena's first meeting at the bohemian bar, just as I had been present at his and Claire's on a beach in Mykonos during a backpacking tour of Europe that we had undertaken together. I could still picture seeing Dennis fixated on her as she walked into the water while we were laid on banana lounges drinking beers with the sound of dance music and audible merriment in the background. As soon as Claire had returned from her swim, he struck up a conversation with the vivacious, blue-eyed Australian girl with long blonde hair. They ended up spending the entirety of that night together and then the next. Claire unleashed an affectionate component to Dennis that I had seldom seen. They became inseparable, moving in together about a year later and tying the knot a few years before Helena and I had married.

'Hi, guys! How are we?' I said, opening the door to greet them as they arrived, hugging them one at a time.

They both returned my salutation and entered the house, making their way down the hallway and into the lounge room where they greeted Helena, who rested Matilda in her arms. Dennis ventured to the kitchen and placed a bottle of wine on the kitchen counter while Helena gave Matilda to an awaiting Claire, resulting in a warm clucky greeting from her. The two women began to conversate as I made my way into the kitchen to speak with Dennis. I grabbed some glasses from the cupboard and he began to pour the wine in front of me. I studied the reasonably tall and slenderly athletic man with somewhat chiselled facial features underneath his freckly complexion. His short, red hair, probably more strawberry blonde than ginger, never really had a style to it, sometimes fixed with a buzzcut, while other times lazily arranged on top with length. Despite the classic prejudice of 'rangas' being somewhat unappealing, he had been quite successful with females in his younger, unattached days. When sober, he could be quite reserved and often unremarkable and those who weren't well-acquainted with him could refer to him as quiet or even shy. However, when lubricated with alcohol, he could transform into a loud, funny, confidently charming man, which was the state that he had met Claire in.

'Busy week, mate?' he enquired.

'Yeah, flat knacker actually. We've been working on Falcone's joint and he's been kicking up a fuss left, right and centre about things. Bloke is doing my head in,' I replied with a shake of my head.

Dennis, a detective with the police, laughed.

'Yes, mate, dealt with him a few times. Not the most pleasant fella in the world.'

'How about you?' I returned.

'Yeah, flat out this week, too,' Dennis answered.

This was his normal manner when it came to work discussions; he was usually very tight-lipped. Although, one night during a drinking session at a pub, lips had seemingly been loosened and he had confided in me about his frustration with the state of the police force that he was part of. He despised the corruption that ran rampant through the force's higher ranks and was livid with the hidden jurisdiction that certain factions of the underworld seemed to have over them. However, this was the only time he had ever extrapolated on those details of his work and they had not been mentioned since. We brought the drinks over to where the women stood in the lounge room and Claire put Matilda down on the floor to allow her to crawl around of her own accord. All four of us joined in with a salute to the end of the working week with a clink and sip of our glasses.

'Helena, dinner smells amazing,' Dennis announced.

'Luckily, Tilly has been really good today so I've had plenty of time up my sleeve to attempt something I've wanted to do for a while. Hope you're all hungry!' Helena replied excitedly, her eyes widening as she talked.

'Bloody starving, don't worry about that,' Dennis said as he tapped his stomach.

'Oh yeah, I've been looking forward to this all day!' added Claire.

'Okay, well why don't you all head to the table and let's eat,' Helena announced as she got up and headed to the kitchen to get the food. 'Jack, can you put Tilly in her high chair?'

I obeyed, clutching a wriggly Matilda and making my way over to the table to place her in position. Helena warmed a bottle of milk in the microwave, whilst Dennis grabbed the serving dish that contained the food and Claire procured some plates and cutlery. I took my place at the table as it was all delivered, with Helena delivering a bottle to Matilda. Everyone sat down and Helena began to dish up the meal in front of hungry eyes that gazed at their plates in an inquisitive excitement. The tune of audible praise and groans of culinary satisfaction at Helena's cooking carried around the table as we all tucked in, inaugurating lively chatter throughout the course of the meal.

After everyone had had their fill, we sat back on our chairs, contentedly stuffed, and reconvened a more focused conversation.

'I can't wait until we have our own little one, Dennis,' Claire mentioned at the dinner table, conveying a mild disappointment for their lack of success in conceiving.

'I know, I know. Hopefully soon,' Dennis replied soothingly as he stretched out his arm and rubbed her back.

'Need it to be a boy so we can get him married to Tilly,' I quipped. 'Although, knowing his dad's ways as a young fella, maybe I don't want her married to him!'

We all shared a chuckle, conceding in the knowledge of Dennis' promiscuity as a young man.

'Oh, get stuffed! You were worse than me! Plus, my young bloke will be hot property, so better tell young Tilly to play her cards right if she wants a crack,' Dennis responded jokingly.

Again, the table laughed.

'Did it take you two long?' Claire enquired, changing the subject to a more serious tone and glancing in Helena's direction.

She turned her head to look at me cheerfully and then back to Claire

'To be truthful, it didn't take us very long at all. Probably a month,' Helena informed. 'But honestly, don't worry. Everyone is different. How long have you been trying?'

'A couple of months,' Claire said, raising her eyebrows and looking at her partner.

'Oh, mate, not all doom and gloom yet. I've actually enjoyed all the trying, happy to keep it up!' he responded with a cheeky grin as he leant back in his chair and surveyed all of our faces.

Claire rolled her eyes with a wry smile.

'It'll happen, no worries about that,' I added and pointed to Matilda in her high chair at the head of the table. 'Just enjoy the sleep-ins while you can. This little bugger doesn't really appreciate a lazy morning!'

'Got that right, but I wouldn't have it any other way,' Helena announced as she left her chair and picked up Matilda. 'Speaking of sleep, I'm gonna put her down. Claire, would you like to help me?'

'Oh, I'd love to!' replied Claire excitedly, leaving her seat.

'Alright, Tilly. Give daddy a kiss,' Helena requested as she brought Matilda over to where I sat.

I planted a kiss on her lips and it was reciprocated by a wet, slobbery one on mine.

'Love you, baby girl,' I said dotingly as I wiped my mouth.

'Night, Till,' added Dennis as he waved in her direction, with the two women leaving in course of Matilda's room.

'Righto, I s'pose that's our cue to clean this up,' I said as we both stood from our chairs and began to clear the dishes. 'You're not worried about that whole baby thing, are you?'

'Nah, mate, not really,' Dennis responded as he stopped what he was doing and looked up with a shake of his head. 'We'll be right. Been pretty happy with a regular root, if I'm being honest!'

'Toey bastard,' I chuckled.

We both picked up the dishes and took them into the kitchen, placing some of them on the counter under my instruction before I stated defiantly that the dishes were tomorrow's problem. We made our way into the lounge room and turned on the television in time for the beginning of the football, with the girls joining us shortly after. They had no interest in watching the football and we had no interest in submitting to being stereotypical males who were unable to engage in dialogue while sport was on, so conversation and wine flowed for most of our time together as the hours ticked by into late evening.

As we waved to our guests from the front veranda on their departure, I put my arm around Helena.

'What do you reckon?' I asked as I raised my eyebrows cheekily.

She looked up at me and laughed as she cottoned on to my brazen enquiry into any prospect of sexual activity.

'I reckon you're in luck, Mr Newton,' she smiled sassily as she pecked my lips, grabbing me by the hand and leading me into our bedroom.

We made love quite passionately. The blaze that had surged before Matilda was born was still well and truly intact for the both of us. In fact, it had never been extinguished. Many couples seemed to squander the tenacity of their passion as their relationship advanced and children were born, but that was not the case for us. We both had a fierce physical attraction to each other and I continued to find her more and more beautiful; she had a hidden sensuality that was veiled by a sweetly tranquil disposition. When it came to bedroom matters, we connected in an effortlessly intense passion; our drives were equally as profound as the others. Afterwards, we lay there, naked in the moonlight that was provided by the uncovered window. So very blissful and so happy in our little world.

Helena slept next to me as my mind ticked over amidst feelings of contented satisfaction, with the thought of my parents running through my head. They had shared many similarities to us; they too were doting parents and very amorous towards one another, so I couldn't help but wonder if this was how joyous married life had been for them before my mother's death. She had passed away from cancer when I was sixteen, having fought a gallant fight throughout, dignified until her last breath. Even when the chemotherapy coursed through her veins, causing her hair to forsake her and malaise to overwhelm her, she was seldom pessimistic. She had a relentlessly positive outlook on life, which had always been her modus operandi right throughout our coexistence as mother and son.

It was an excruciating time for both my father and I; he was never the same. After her death, he lost the will to exist in a normal life as his job went unattended and he proceeded to halt all contact with the outside world. His employer eventually freed him of the burden of employment, resulting in my once brilliant father engaging in copious amounts of drinking at home to numb his pain. The house was usually devoid of light; I think that he had wanted the darkness to mirror that of his soul. He proceeded to tumble into a deep pit of depression and ceased caring about anything, including me. I no longer had a father, just a fellow occupant of a loveless house. The man I knew was gone and only a soulless shell of a human remained. I never felt the tender embrace of love from him again. Eventually, I gave up trying to help him and left home. I would visit to see how Dad was doing but the story was always the same. Drunk or asleep. He was in too deep – even professional help was worthless. He had simply given up. Our relationship consisted of unreciprocated formalities for a few years on my behalf until I determined that it was time to let him be and left him to his own devices.

Mum's death also tainted my fundamental beliefs quite severely, having been a reasonably pious attendee of a Catholic school as an adolescent. Until then, I had never questioned the existence of a god. I had believed that he took care of everyone and had a path planned for them, working in mysterious ways to help all of those on their designation. He had his will and we never questioned it. But then Mum died and I began to question how his mysterious ways were factored into that. It seemed quite sadistic really, the fact that this almighty, transcendent, omnipotent being had allowed my innocent mum to not only die but also suffer. The dogmatic response to these questions was always quashed with one word: faith. And if a follower's finite mind couldn't comprehend an aspect of the religion, or in fact, science provided a contradiction, they were simply told to have faith that the dogma rang true and all was how God wanted things to be. I couldn't buy it any longer. I became agnostic; open to the possibility of there being a higher power but also realistic to the likelihood that there was most likely not. As a result,

Helena and I, who were both similarly versed, chose to live our lives and raise our progeny as good wholesome people, rather than subscribe to any belief system. People seem to question, and indeed fear, their existence in the universe as they search for its meaning. Sometimes, accepting the pointlessness of it all can be a form of liberation and an antidote to the confusion. It was for me.

Chapter 5
This Is the Sound of Settling

With the weekend upon me, I ventured to the local football club to congregate with a few of my friends and view the senior game on display. None of us played any longer but we derived great pleasure from observing and socialising at the club nonetheless. Also, we had become scattered about Melbourne, so it was a nice central location in which to reacquaint ourselves fortnightly when the team hosted a home game. I had played for the side last season and was the last of our collective group to reach cessation from the gruelling game of Australian rules football. After many years of injuries, my body had become increasingly ignorant to the requirements of it and with the continuous advent of younger players, I had determined that my footballing life had arrived at its expiration and entered into retirement. It had also been an appropriate sacrifice with a baby on the way. Although, admittedly, the move from partaking to watching those partake had initially been a difficult transition, given how much football had been a great love of mine throughout my life.

Originally, just like any kid, I had dreamed of making it as a professional and would spend every spare moment with a football glued to my hand. However, despite the fact that I was a skilful player at a junior level, I was not proficient enough to make it professionally. So, when the reality of this dream had become obvious that it was not to eventuate, I focused on becoming a virtuous senior footballer at a local level. Unluckily, to my constant dismay, I was never able to exact my full potential in this realm, due to a mildly tumultuous career laden with injuries. Still, I was satisfied with my time as a player and had no regrets, having extracted the best that I could out of my frail body. I finally enjoyed attending as a spectator, no longer burdened by a desire to be out on the field with the team.

I arrived at the ground in which the club was situated, just after 2 p.m., at the beginning of the first quarter of the match. It was a classically suburban oval, with large club rooms that bejewelled one end of the ground behind the goals, while a kids' playground festooned the opposite end. Along one wing of the oval ran a car park and main road, while along the opposite wing was a creek. The sky displayed a mild gloom and a stiff wind gusted to one end, making conditions seem moderately colder than the forecast. The echo of shouts at the excitement of play rung in the atmosphere, along with the high-pitched screeches of officiating whistles and the occasional expletive or derogatory term inflicted at an opposition player or umpire. People of all ages and walks of life flourished around the boundary of the ground – families convened on picnic rugs, women congregated on deck chairs, men stood in large groups with beers in hand, while children roamed freely about, kicking footballs or playing on the playground.

The aroma of snags, burgers and onions on the barbie perfumed the air as I located the boys amongst the sea of buzzing people in the traditional spot, near to where they had a 'tinny' bar in operation for the masses to purchase beer. My three friends, all of which were school companions, were all of a similar mid-thirty-something age to me and plonked in an analogously settled phase of life. We had faced together, and then bid adieu to, the days of partying and nightclubs, the pursuit of women, and the solitary, unattached lives that we had all appreciated as younger men. We had all progressed to find life partners who had evidently stamped out our inherent male immaturity, with their seemingly innate drive to aid the men whom they deemed partner-worthy to evolve into a more suitable fatherly prototype. However, when placed all together, our maturity levels could revert as we relished unperturbed, giving rise to an infectious immaturity that could affect us all.

The man that stood closest to me was the most subtle of the group, John 'Pilks' Pilkington, whose large hands dwarfed the can of beer that he sipped. He was a tall man, athletically built and the best sportsman of us all, having actually played professional football for a decent portion of his adult life. He had short brown hair that was procured by a cap, with a chiselled jaw and a bulkily protruding nose. Pilks was an inhabitant of a trendy lifestyle, working as a graphic designer in the city for a brewery and uninhibited by any children of his own. This left him free to be occupied with his urban vices, which included frequenting hipster coffee spots, trendy restaurants and farmers markets. Next to him was the smallest man of the group, Marty Bews, or 'Bewsy', who was draped in a woolly scarf to combat the wintriness. In his previous life, he had been a fit individual, quite muscular for his smaller frame, but with the addition of love and career, great sacrifice had come at the weight of his physical pursuits. He had encountered his well-matched partner a short while before I had crossed paths with Helena, which had instigated a rapid leap into a more subdued lifestyle. He had enjoyed partying and the single life as much as anyone, but something about her had rendered him dumbstruck and unveiled an aspect of him that I had seldom glimpsed, even with other partners. A softer bodily physique graced his dark, squirrel-like features, with his black hair and eyebrows framing his face characteristically. He could be the most rambunctious of the group, given it took diminutive amounts of alcohol to morph him into a comically drunken state; however, with this said, alcohol was not a prerequisite of his to appear engaging in a social situation, as he was easily the most outgoing and socially inclined of us all. Next to Bewsy stood Mark Peters, whom we called 'Chewie', a similarly rambunctiously natured man, especially when furnished with alcohol and in the comfortable presence of his friends. He was a man of similar height to me but less athletically inclined in both ability and appearance, with a bulbous-shaped head that was adorned with brown hair in the midst of receding and obscured by a grey, knitted beanie. He was always smartly attired with fashionably expensive clothing, a nod to his more affluent status compared to us all. Chewie was the only one apart from myself who was with child and married, but given he lived a moderate distance outside of the city, he was the friend that I saw the least of.

'G'day, boys!' I remarked, greeting them with handshakes that progressed into hugs as they all received me cheerfully.

'Here's your tinny,' Pilks said, distributing a beer to me.

'You beauty. Thank you,' I replied, inserting it into the stubby holder that I had brought from home. 'How are we all, anyway?'

The concise responses to my rudimentary question varied as we watched the game unfold excitedly.

'How's the guns on that bloke?' I exclaimed, referring to the muscular ruckman on the field for the other team who was decorated with immense biceps.

'Reminds me of the pipes I had in my heyday,' Bewsy said facetiously with a smirk.

'Yeah, shame you're fat as a house now!' Chewie joked, moving his hand to jeeringly tap Bewsy's stomach.

'I could still belt you though!' Bewsy said while placing Chewie in a playful headlock as we all chuckled.

'You missing playing at all, Jacko?' Pilks took a mouthful of his beer.

'Yeah, nah, not really anymore. My body was cactus last year so I'm pretty happy not to feel so sore anymore. Probably miss socialising at the footy club the most,' I answered. 'How 'bout you?'

'Not one bit.' Pilks leered as I smiled at his response.

'How's work been going?' I asked before I sipped my drink.

'Same old, really,' he replied. 'Been pretty flat out with a few bits and pieces but still really enjoying it. You?'

'Oh, mate, still dealing with old mate Rocco Falcone,' I responded as they all laughed, aware of his reputation and having heard my ramblings previously. 'He's such a flog! I tell you, it's nice to get on the piss after the week I've had dealing with him.'

'Pretty schmick joint he's got though,' Bewsy added. 'Plus, he'd be splashing some serious kanga around, I would've thought, so it would still be an enjoyable job though, wouldn't it?'

A thunderous cheer broke out from the home crowd that we were nestled amongst, as one of the players slotted an impressive goal from the boundary. Our conversation halted momentarily as we marvelled in his efforts along with the excited masses.

'Yeah, design-wise it's been brilliant, actually. Gonna look grouse once we're done – I'm pretty rapt in my design. That is, if I don't throw a couple of cut lunches and knock him out before that.'

'I would love to have a sticky beak at that house,' remarked Pilks. 'I've been past a few times but that massive fence stops you from seeing anything!'

'Mate, it's a real monstrosity from the outside, but the inside is pretty impressive,' I said, as I took another swig of my can. 'Actually, how's your house coming along, Chewie?'

'Real good thanks, Jacko.' He crumpled the empty beer can that he held in his hand. 'The joint was a bit of a dog's brekkie when we got it but kitchen and ensuite have come up an absolute treat. Now, just gotta finish the bathroom and she's pretty much done. When it's all done and dusted, we'll have all you up there for a barbie.'

'I'm not coming up there to have a barbie with all your yobbo mates!' Bewsy said.

'Oh, righto, well we don't need dills like you there anyway!' Chewie said, mischievously nudging Bewsy in the ribs.

'And you reckon you're not feral, Bewsy? Turn it up!' Pilks pushed him away playfully.

'It's okay, Pilks, if he doesn't come, I'll save on meat anyway because the little porky bastard won't be there to pinch all the tucker!' Chewie cried with laughter as all of snickered.

'Give me a spell,' Bewsy returned. 'You've got a head like a beaten favourite and you're losing the feathers on top of it!'

'I didn't realise you were Brad Pitt,' Chewie quipped.

'Practically twins,' Bewsy joked.

'Mate, you've got no idea,' Chewie responded. 'You're not the full quid, I swear!'

The duo exchanged a grin as we continued to watch the play, the roar of the zealous crowd interposing our drolly puerile commentary of each other's lives.

'How's the misso, Bewsy?' I eventually quizzed.

'Yeah, not bad, Jacko. She's still pushing to start a family. I'm not sure I'm ready. I love my life the way it is. I can nick off and go surfing on the weekends or we can travel when we want and I'm in a good spot career-wise. Also, we'd probably have to get a bigger house and I don't really have a brass razoo to my name at the moment. Plus, she wants me to give up the darts!'

We chortled in unison at his last statement, knowing how much he loved a smoke in a social situation or to cope with the stresses of his job.

'Well, giving up the durries is a good thing, nuffy,' I informed. 'But to be honest, mate, you're never a hundred per cent ready for kids. I know I wasn't.'

'Bloody oath, you're never ready.' Chewie chuckled. 'Plus, we all know you're batting above your average there, Sir Donald. So do what she says, I reckon!'

'Good call,' Pilks added as we all laughed.

'But seriously, it's the best thing I've ever done,' I said after the cackling ceased.

The day continued as we revelled in the enjoyment of the schoolboy banter and comradery, which lasted for the remainder of the match and covered varying topics while we tipped in a few beers. After my former team was victorious in a hard-fought victory, I made my way home with a slight feeling of merriment, possibly flirting with the legal limit for blood alcohol. Even though the rule of thumb for us was one can per quarter of the match, I still felt a bit pissed before getting into the car to drive. By the time I got home, I was quite lethargic due to the amalgamation of alcohol and a winter's day. I made my way into the house to greet my girls and feigned sobriety to my wife before laying ecstatically prone on the couch. I remained there for much of the evening and enjoyed a cosy Saturday night within the walls of our humble abode, happily emancipated from any engagement with the outside world and in the company of the two most important people in the world to me.

Chapter 6
Sunday Bloody Sunday

A miserably raucous cry that emanated from Matilda's bedroom jolted me into consciousness the next morning. Helena stirred in response but after I reassured her that I would heed the call, she went back to sleep. I arose and headed into Tilly's room, opening the door to view her standing upright in her cot with tears streaming down her chubby cheeks; her delicate face showed a despondency that made me feel an obvious sense of parental sympathy for my little girl.

'Oh, Tilly, what's wrong?' I soothed gently as I scooped her up in my arms.

She bawled as I swayed back and forth with her in an attempt to provide reassurance. Her bleary green eyes sparkled as I gazed at them lovingly and began to sing an old nostalgia-laced Australian folk tune that I had fond memories of my mother singing to me as a child.

'Give me a home amongst the gum trees, with lots of plumb trees. A sheep or two and a kangaroo, a clothesline out the back, veranda out the front and an old rocking chair.'

Matilda ceased her crying and looked up at me. For whatever reason, this song was usually successful in mollifying any sadness that she had. I then administered her dummy, in which she audibly slurped away on, seemingly happily pacified.

'That's better, little grub, isn't it?' I asked rhetorically as I held her in my arms. 'Come on, let's go and make mummy some brekkie, shall we?'

The both of us then moved into the kitchen and I began to construct the ritualistic Sunday morning fry-up of bacon, eggs and toast. Whilst cooking, I couldn't help but cast my mind back to the Sundays of the past, situated in a seemingly far-gone era of my youth. In those days, the Sundays that followed a night or weekend of heavy consumption could be a rough experience. I would refer to them as the Sunday blues; the days where the clouds seemed to gather around me to make the light in my world duller. They were days where life felt arduously bleak and the 'black dog' would visit, spending hours or days by my side. The worst part was the sense of unknown as to when the feeling would forsake; some days, it felt as if life might never return to a normal serenity. At the time, it was just seen as something that was par for the course if I wanted to indulge in life's vices of drugs and alcohol. But, in the wake of hindsight, I wasn't sure why I had put myself through it. If anything, it made me so sincerely thankful for the pure bliss that Sundays had become; it was a day with my family that I truly relished.

Following her small lie-in, Helena joined us, half-asleep, at the kitchen table to enjoy the fruits of my culinary labour. She squinted with the advent of light; like me, she wasn't the greatest morning person. I gifted her with a coffee, which she received gratefully before quietly munching away on her toast. The melody of my morning playlist softly resonated throughout the frigid house, with the wintry morning sun poking a radiance through the windows that was unable to provide a warming touch to the skin. Despite exchanging fleeting words, we both basked in the enjoyment of a pleasure as simple as a nice breakfast that was complemented with the promise of a lovely day. Following our meal, the three of us made our way to Princes Park, which was a vast sprawl of an urban landscape in Carlton, containing lusciously green-grassed ovals, bordered by large canopies of trees. The area was encircled by a popular running track for people to frequent, populated with individuals from all manners of existence who were engaging in the crisp day that had been provided. It was brisk but not intolerably cold by any stretch of the imagination – a sort of cold, where if one was rugged up sufficiently like we were, it was quite enjoyably refreshing. No breeze was felt on the skin and a thin cloud cover provided a nice shade from the weakened winter sun but afforded a bright light in which to engage in the day's activities. Helena and I found ourselves at one of the children's playgrounds that speckled the perimeter of the parkland, pushing Matilda on the swing. She looked utterly adorable, dressed in a pink jacket and furry beanie, beaming with joy as she experienced the thrill of a change in velocity that children appeared to enjoy much more valiantly than most of their adult counterparts. Following her jaunt on the swing, we relocated Matilda back to her pram and engaged in an expedition around the track, amidst all of the walkers and runners.

'I really miss running,' I said as we began our stroll, referring to the joggers that hustled past us at varying paces.

'Well, why don't you get back in to it?' Helena replied curiously.

'I feel guilty. Don't get me wrong, the favourite part of my day is walking in the front door and seeing you two, but I stopped exercising because I'd feel guilty if I was to go for a run and you'd been home with her all day. Seems a bit selfish on my behalf.'

'Oh, you absolute dag! That mind never stops ticking, does it? I really love that you thought of me but I want you to be happy, too! I know how much you love your fitness and I know how much you miss playing footy. You gave that up for us so I don't want you to stop doing what makes you happy all together. We all need an outlet to blow off some steam, babe.'

She moved one of her hands to rub my back as I smiled contently, pushing the pram along.

'Well, what about you?' I asked after a slight pause, with the sound of the stroller and our footsteps moving over the gravel path to become more audible in the silence.

'What about me?' she returned.

'Well, you're with her all day, without a break. Wouldn't you like an outlet? Wouldn't you prefer me to come home and take her off your hands?'

'Oh, Jacko. We're in this together. You work hard to give us the greatest life. And when you get home, you're the most amazing dad and husband. Honestly, I'm playing my part by taking care of her and really living my dream of being a mum right now. So, if you ask me if I ever really feel like I need a break, no, I don't. I'm living my life so happily right now and I want my partner in crime to do the same.'

She touched me lovingly on the shoulder as I gazed affectionately in her direction and mouthed the words 'I love you'.

'I love you too,' she whispered with a smile, pausing for a moment and then adding in a facetious tone, 'Plus, we can't have you getting fat on me now!'

We both chuckled as we journeyed on.

'Is this how you pictured our life was gonna be?' I asked after a few seconds.

She looked forward for an instant as she pondered the question with the gravelly sounds emanating from below our feet as we made our way.

'Yes. I always imagined that we'd live somewhere around here and live our life the way we do. Mostly, I always thought we'd be happy and really just have a fun, easy, simple life. And I really think we have all of that. I know I wouldn't change a thing for the world.'

I moved a hand off the pram and put my arm around her, drawing her closer and kissing her on the head as we continued to walk.

'Me either, not for quids.'

After completing a lap of the track, we made our way from the park to a local pub for lunch. It was here that we met Helena's sister Lucy and her partner Bryan in an impressively gentrified area of the inner-city suburb of Fitzroy. Once upon a time, the corner pub would have been filled largely with rugged, blue-collar characters, eagerly consuming pots of beer and smoking cigarettes after a long day of laborious toil. Nowadays, the charming double-storey façade with cambered windows was neatly rendered and painted in a cream colour, full of individuals and families of a more affluent and sophisticated manner. Inside, the floor that would have been marinated in litres of spilt ale and cigarette ash in its past life, thanks to the rambunctious patrons, was now a fancier polished concrete, with a gleamingly refurbished timber bar that lived in the centre of the rectangular room. The walls of the pub were a trendy exposed brick adorned with countless articles of memorabilia from the Fitzroy football club, the team that resided closest to my heart. I had grown up passionately barracking for them, due to the fact that my father and late grandfather had been fervent supporters, even throughout their merger with the Brisbane Bears and subsequent relocation to Brisbane in the 1990s.

I had begun to initiate the brainwashing early on Matilda, as my father had done to me, gifting her a football jumper at birth and frequently serenading her with the club theme song. Not that this was really necessary, given that Helena and her family weren't exactly sportingly inclined. As we entered the pub, it was busy with activity, abuzz with general merriment of punters and the prominent sound of football commentary of the Sunday game, which today featured Brisbane. I pushed Matilda's pram through the crowd and we found our way to a corner of the tavern where we located our lunchtime companions. I greeted Bryan with a handshake, a pleasantly smiley Māori man with dark hair and facial features. I then moved to receive Lucy, a woman with light brown hair, who was not as tall or slender as her sister, but shared evident genetic similarities. Together they formed a highly agreeable company and I endeared them both for their congenially warm dispositions.

We sat at the table across from them as Lucy took Matilda out of her pram and wrapped her up in a big cuddle, planting numerous kisses on her face. Bryan smiled glowingly at her.

'How have you two been?' Helena eventually asked when Lucy had stopped clucking at Tilly.

'Yeah, really good,' Lucy said as Bryan gleefully nodded in agreeance. 'Just busy with life. How about you guys?'

'Yeah, us too,' Helena replied. 'She keeps us busy!'

'I'll grab us some drinks,' I announced as I left my chair. 'What do we all want?'

'Beer's fine for me,' Helena said.

'Same. Thanks, Jack,' responded Lucy appreciatively.

'Cheers, mate,' answered Bryan, indicating his compliance.

I moved to the bar and shortly returned with four pots of Carlton Draught and some menus for lunch. I already knew that I would be having a chicken parma but the others usually seemed to be more willing to vary their orders than me. The table thanked me and Lucy announced an obligatory 'cheers' as we clanked our glasses before all taking a sip.

'How's work, Jack?' she then asked after a nip of her beer.

'Yeah, pretty good thanks, Luce,' I responded. 'We're flat out at the moment, actually. My business partner has just left for a holiday to Bali so I'll be even busier this week.'

'Oh, well, they might bump into Mum and Dad over there,' Lucy said.

'I'm not sure if your mum and dad would be keen on these two.' I smirked. 'Don't get me wrong, I love them both, but I think they would probably be your classic, cringeworthy, Aussie bogans in Bali.'

The table laughed and Helena nodded agreeingly.

'Have you spoken to Mum and Dad?' Helena then asked Lucy.

'Yeah, once or twice,' she responded. 'They sound like they're having a ball, don't they?'

'Yeah, they're so funny,' Helena said merrily. 'Mum is so paranoid about getting Bali belly!'

'Oh, I know.' Lucy laughed. 'You know how she is.'

Yeah, a little pedantic and over the top, I chuckled internally as I had another taste of my beer.

'When are they back again?' Helena asked. 'Is it Saturday?'

'Yeah, Saturday,' Lucy confirmed.

My attention was then averted to the football on the television and away from the girl's conversation as the teams commenced their run out onto the field for the imminently starting game. The girls took the conversation down their own path, while Bryan and I were left to our own devices to engage in chit-chat. Bryan, being from New Zealand, was more inclined to rugby rather than football, but he would usually ask questions as to appear interested, which I greatly appreciated.

'How you been anyway, mate?' Bryan suddenly asked in his prominent Kiwi accent.

'Yeah, really good, mate,' I replied as I diverted my eyes from the nearby television screen and looked at the man across from me. 'What's news with you?'

'Nah, nothing much, Jack. Same old stuff.'

'Yeah, it gets a bit that way, doesn't it? You need a bloody holiday.'

'We've decided we're going to Auckland this year for Christmas, so that'll be nice.'

'Ah, beauty. Your old lady will be rapt, not sure if theirs will though!'

We both chortled, as we glanced back up to the television screen.

'Hang on, did I hear that correctly?' Helena re-joined.

'Can you stop sticky-beaking in our convo, please?' I reacted facetiously.

'Yeah, you heard right,' Lucy answered as Bryan grinned. 'We decided the other day.'

'Mum's gonna chuck a wobbly!' Helena laughed.

'Oh, god, I know. Can you imagine!' Lucy chuckled. 'But we haven't been to New Zealand for Chrissy, ever. It's only fair.'

'Yeah, definitely,' Helena agreed. 'But Mum will be flat as a tack. You know the big deal she likes to put on for Chrissy day.'

'I'll get golden boy to tell her,' Lucy joked, smirking at Bryan.

'Team effort,' he countered smilingly.

'Bloody brilliant for me,' I added. 'Now I might be a chance to be number one son-in-law!'

The table giggled with the full knowledge of how much she adored Bryan.

'Come on, she loves you both equally,' Helena said.

'Pig's arse!' I cheekily countered. 'I'm a firm second.'

'Oh, well, we'll be there to deal with all the relos,' Helena declared with a roll of her eyes.

'We don't exactly have any opposition from my side of the family,' I stated irreverently.

'How is your dad going?' Lucy quizzed. 'Do you hear from him at all?'

'Nope, not a whisper,' I replied. 'I did ring him to let him know that he had a granddaughter but he didn't answer and never replied to the message that I left on the answering machine. So, I don't really know how he's going. I can only presume.'

'Sad,' Lucy sympathised.

'Is he still drinking and that?' Bryan asked.

'I would presume so,' I said. 'Honestly, we haven't spoken in a long time and I haven't been to his place in yonks.'

'Well, we used to pop in for his birthday and Christmas and give him a little present,' Helena informed, 'but he never really seemed that rapt to see us. So, we then just started to leave a pressie on his doorstep with a nice card but we never got a thank you from him or anything, not that that matters. But after a little while, we decided to just leave him be.'

'Look, don't get me wrong, I hope he's well,' I said, 'but you can only try so much to be there for him and help him. When Mum died, I tried so hard to help. And then we tried to be part of his life but he didn't want it. It gets exhausting and to a point where you can't do it anymore when you're getting nothing in return. It's fine, I have my own family and I love being part of yours.'

'Well, it's his loss, Jack, because you're an asset to our family.' Lucy beamed warmly.

'Thanks, Luce,' I said a little embarrassedly as Helena put her hand lovingly on my thigh.

'Yeah, I don't mind having you round either,' Helena drolly added.

Helena and I shared a playful smile as we let the moment pass.

'Alright, enough of this lovey-dovey stuff,' I interjected. 'Back to the footy.'

'I'll order for us then,' Helena said as she left the table. 'Can't have my big strong asset going hungry now, can I? I'm guessing parma, Jack?'

I turned to look up at her and gave a cheeky wink, which she returned as she left for the bar.

'I'll do the same,' Lucy advised. 'What do you want, Kiwi?'

'Steak, thanks,' Bryan replied as she departed and we both turned to the football on the television screen. 'How you blokes gonna go this year?'

'We'll be thereabouts, I reckon,' I replied, averting my eyes from the screen in front of us. 'Got rid of a bit of the riff-raff that was clogging our list and recruited a few gun players so I'm quietly confident in us making the finals this year.'

'Nice.'

'How about your rugby team?'

'They're going alright but I find it hard to follow it here. Back home it's on the telly or in the pubs, but here it's never on. I stream some games but it's not the same.'

'It's tough in Oz. I mean, rugby union here is like a third-tier sport. You've got footy and cricket, rugby league, even soccer. Plus, it's been so mismanaged I don't even know how they would begin to make it big again. Shame, I s'pose.'

'I've come to terms with it. I spend my time here with you watching footy more anyway.'

'Maybe you've just seen the light and found a decent sport.'

'Piss off!'

I laughed as Helena appeared back at the table, with another pot of beer in her hand.

'What's this?' I asked as she placed it in front of me.

'Pot and parma,' she informed. 'I know you love a good deal.'

'Looks like you're driving home,' I joked as I took a big sip of my original beer.

The day proceeded very well from there, with a thoroughly

enjoyable chicken parma to go along with a few pots of Carlton Draught. Most importantly, the mighty Lions got up to win the match as we shouted at the telly and cheered them on. We made our way home after farewelling Bryan and Lucy, with all of us a little weary after the busy day. As a result, the evening consisted of Helena and I pottering around the house and performing menial tasks until it was an acceptable time to put Matilda to sleep and head to bed ourselves.

I had always found Sunday nights such a bittersweet time, as they mixed a feeling of joy with a feeling of dread at the anticipation of the working days ahead. However, that night the sensation was lessened by the fact that I would have the office to myself for the week; an impending sense of freedom cushioned any ill feelings to provide me with an optimism that rocked me to a comfy sleep.

III.

If I am the tide,

then she is the moon.

The celestial in my sky

that guides me through.

If offered an eternity,

it would be too soon.

Infinite forevers,

would be too few.

Chapter 7
Soul Meets Body

Following the chat that I'd had with Helena the day before, regarding the neglection of my fitness, I decided that Monday was the day to instigate some form of campaign. I returned home from work and greeted the girls before quickly retiring to the bedroom to put some running gear on.

It was important for me to exercise as soon as I got home after a long day because I tended to be inundated with lethargy, along with a flurry of self-imposed excuses, if I didn't. I'd invited Ted to come along for a run with me; for one, I needed the distraction from the pain that I was about to feel, and secondly, I needed motivation from an outside source. Ted was a naturally gifted endurance athlete, who would drag me along at a pace that I would not allow myself to reach if I was to run solo.

I heard him pull up on the street shortly after I was changed and left the house to greet him. His blue eyes and kind features smiled at me as I shook his hand. He sported his mousy, slightly greying hair quite scruffily, dressed in a long-sleeve top under a training singlet of a football club that he had previously played for in Adelaide. The attire displayed his lean yet powerfully built physique and also the undeniable fact that he was a highly proficient footballer, who had arguably been thwarted from a professional career due to his smaller stature. As we stood in the street, the wintertime light was fading into dusk, with a mild wintry breeze that was not too cold or strong enough to be a hindrance whilst running.

'G'day, mate,' I warmly addressed him.

'G'day, cobber,' he returned.

'We ready to do this?'

'Are you?'

'It's not gonna be pretty. We all know I'm built for power, not endurance.'

Ted chortled. 'I reckon we should have a stretch first. Don't want you to ping a calf or hammy!'

'Yeah, good call,' I said as we proceeded to the tree on the nature strip and began to stretch our calves.

'How'd your day pan out without Georgey and Elaine?' Ted strained as he grimaced from the stretching.

'Real well actually. Got plenty done. So bloody nice and peaceful in the office. How'd you go?'

Ted rolled his eyes and sneered as I followed up my question. 'Rocco?'

'Yep.'

'Cunt?'

'Yep. Absolute genuine cunt.'

We both laughed and shook our heads as we moved to touch our toes to stretch our hamstrings, both groaning in the process.

'How's the hugs and kisses?' I asked a little breathlessly.

'Yeah, good thanks, mate. She's working nights at the moment so she's pretty happy for me not to be at home until she wakes up. I have to tip-toe around the house when I get home from work until about dinner time, or else she wakes up real grumpy and absolutely cracks the shits! So, this is perfect, mate. I usually get out a few times a week when I'm not training for footy so I'd be happy to tow you along for a plod whenever you'd like.'

'That would be nice. Righto, how far you wanna go?'

'We'll go for five Ks. Not too fast. I'll take it easy on you.'

I exhaled loudly – even five kilometres sounded daunting to a man that hadn't run in over six months and was not naturally inclined to endurance running.

'Alright, lead us off.' I sighed.

Ted fiddled with his wristwatch for a moment with a short flurry of beeps and then announced that the run was to begin. We set off at a kind pace and floated around the suburb in a route that was dictated by him. Past the old-fashioned yet endearing houses that lined the suburb and housed the working class, some in need of amity, while others had been graced with grateful owners who had restored them to their deserved splendour. Past the lots that had fallen to the tyranny of development and suburb gentrification, some empty blocks, while some were in the midst of a transformation that epitomised the slow death of character at the advent of utilitarian buildings. Past the boggy yet green grassed ovals of the local sporting ground, whose huge light towers beamed down upon the children who trained enthusiastically on the ovals. We ran briskly into the dusk light, overtaking people out walking, who scrambled to get out of the way of the two burly figures that passed them. Personally, the first few minutes of the run were okay, but after that period, it descended into a lot of heavy breathing with the aid of my burning lungs. Ted barely broke a sweat, while I more resembled a wounded beast, gasping for air before it succumbed to its injuries. I spluttered around, trying to keep up with him and reply to his occasional comments or questions. I couldn't help but wonder why fitness faded so rapidly and didn't just get to a point where it stayed forever. However, these were most likely ramblings of a brain that was starved of oxygen, rather than any profound intuitions or philosophy. We eventually made it back to Harvist Street and concluded the run out the front of the house. Ted pressed his watch and respired mildly strenuously, while I inhaled and exhaled loudly to suck in some heavy breaths.

'You okay, big fella?' Ted sniggered. 'Don't die on me.'

I attempted a laugh, which sounded more like a strained and wheezing exhale.

'Fuck me dead, I am unfit.' I gasped.

'Yeah, the rig looks a bit softer than I remember,' Ted jeered, 'but you're still in decent nick at least for a married bloke with a tin lid. Most blokes are happy to blow out and get a bit muddy.'

'Thanks, mate. I think,' I said with another panting laugh as we both made our way to sit on the veranda in the gloomy evening light.

'How's Tilly?'

'Good as gold. She's an absolute little ripper, that girl.'

'Yeah, me and the misso are trying actually.'

'You beauty! Good on ya, mate.'

'Thanks, Jacko. We're both super excited about it.'

'It's the best, mate. It consumes your life and changes absolutely everything, but it's grouse. I'm excited for you both. Best of luck.'

'Cheers, ledge,' Ted replied as he got up from the veranda. 'I better go and get some dinner to bring home to the darl then. Need a hand up?'

I looked up at him and nodded with a wry smile as he reached out his hand to grab mine and pulled me up, both of us straining with the effort.

'I think I might be a touch sore tomorrow,' I groaned.

'I reckon!' Ted laughed as he made his way to his car. 'See you later, mate.'

'Hooroo, Teddy. Thanks for that.' I saluted from the front yard.

I waved at him as he drove away and ventured inside the house where I was greeted by Helena and Matilda in the living area.

'How did you go?' Helena asked eagerly from the kitchen.

'It wasn't pretty,' I said as I bent down and kissed Matilda, who was playing on the floor.

'Oh, well, at least you're back into it,' Helena soothed.

'Yeah, for sure,' I responded as I made my way to the kitchen and moved towards her.

'Jack, don't you dare!' she screamed playfully with a wide-eyed expression before I wrapped her in a sweaty hug. 'Yuck! Get off me!'

She tried to resist my clutches as I cackled and held her for a moment before letting go.

'Get in the shower, you filthy man!' She grinned impishly as she friskily hit me a few times with the tea towel that she was holding.

'I'm on my way!' I replied as I turned and headed to the bedroom for a shower.

After dinner, we put Matilda down to bed and enjoyed some time on the couch, curled up together. I loved the evenings when it was just us two because, in reality, it was really the only time that we had alone collectively, apart from sleep. Sometimes we would watch documentaries or certain television series, while other times we would just sit enveloped within each other and talk on the couch. That night, we sat with cups of tea cooling on the coffee table and engaged in the latter, both quite tiresome from our daily adventures.

'Oh, I forgot to tell you, Ted and Laura are trying for a baby,' I mentioned as I looked down at Helena who was curled up into me.

'Oh, wow, how exciting for them,' she replied as she sat up and grabbed her tea from the coffee table. 'Must be something in the air because it seems to be the in-vogue thing at the moment, doesn't it?'

I nodded with a half-smile as she took a sip of her camomile blend.

'Be nice for Til to have some friends to grow up with,' I added after a moment.

Helena paused and appeared to consider something as she puffed on the small amount of steam that rose from her cup.

'Or a little sister or brother,' she stated as she looked at me searchingly.

I gazed at Helena with a look of surprise. We had both always stated that more than one child was an inevitability, but to that point, we had not discussed when we would start trying again for another. I think that I had just been waiting for her to be ready for it, given my part in the pregnancy was reasonably negligible.

'Yeah, a boy would be great,' I answered mischievously, glowing excitedly at the prospect.

She glanced at me, wide-eyed, before placing her mug next to mine on the coffee table.

'I think I'm ready to start trying, Jack,' she said tenderly as she placed her hand on mine. 'What do you think?'

'I think I'd like to start trying too,' I muttered.

Helena leant forward and wrapped her arms around my neck before planting a tender kiss on my lips. We gazed into each other's eyes for a moment without a word being said, pausing in pure happiness and savouring the feeling for all that it was worth. It was then that Helena instigated a more amorous kiss and we began to grip each other tighter and more passionately as our breathing became heavier and movements more lustful. She then pulled away and rose from the couch before reaching for my hand to clutch it.

'Can we start now?' she whispered softly before leading me to the bedroom.

If she was the moon, then I was the tide.

Chapter 8
The Italian Job

The sound of talkback radio punctuated my drive the next morning as I made the short journey to work. It was a lovely sunny morning, the warming rays made me feel a grateful joy to have the office to myself, beckoned by the tantalising offer of freedom and solitude that I was ill-afforded at home. I pulled up at the back of the building and parked the car, getting out with a groan of pain that resonated from my aggrieved body. As I entered the office, my phone buzzed in my pocket. I pulled it out and glanced at the screen to see an unknown number as the door clicked shut behind me.

'Hello, Jack Newton speaking.'

'G'day Jack, my name's Tony Antonello. How you going, mate?'

'Going well, Tony. What can I do for you?'

'Well, mate, I'm a friend of Rocco's. He said you've been doing some work for him and recommended your company to me, actually.'

'Oh, right, yeah, been doing the big reno at his place for him.'

'Yeah, that's right. Well, I'm a developer and I've just bought a massive plot of land. I've used big firms in the past but I'm wanting to change tact and go through one of the little blokes because I think you'll be much easier to deal with. Anyway, I'd like to talk to you about working on the project for me.'

'Oh, right, yeah, that sounds interesting. How big is the development?'

'Well, if you're not busy tonight for dinner, I'd like to go over it with you.'

'Cool, um, I'll have to check with the missus first. We have a baby at home that we'll have to get minded.'

'Bring your wife and if no one can mind the little one, I'll pay for a babysitter.'

'That's very generous of you, Tony, but I think we should be able to find someone.'

'Great. Do you know my restaurant, Truffatore?'

'Yes, of course.'

'Meet me there at 7 p.m. Just mention your names at the door and they'll bring you up to me.'

'Okay, Tony, great. I'll see you then.'

'Righto, Jack. See you then, mate.'

I hung up the phone in a mild disbelief. I knew exactly who Tony Antonello was, and so did the majority of the general public. He was infamous, usually in the papers for brushes with the law or seen wining and dining in the presence of less than reputable characters like Rocco. I knew that he was a big developer; his company had been part of some impressively huge developments around the city. However, he was always seemingly dogged by a gangster reputation and was reportedly less than Kocher in the way that he conducted himself.

I rang Helena to inform her of our newly acquired plans, of which she shared a mutually wary excitement before acquiescing to the invitation and advising me that she would find a babysitter. After hanging up, I journeyed down the long corridor, reflecting on the morning's events that swirled in my head to form a mild dilemma. I was torn; the job was likely to be financially rewarding, which would make it hard to pass up, but I deliberated about whether I wanted to work with clients with such notoriety and become embedded somewhere that I didn't want to exist. I could've been unwillingly accepting a poison chalice, while on the other hand, my overthinking could've led me to pass up a fantastic opportunity for not only my business but also my family.

I worked at the front desk for the rest of the morning, during which I had to constantly remind myself to not overthink the dinner invitation. The sound of soft, wordless music echoed around the empty office as I grew jealous of the sunshine that stared back at me from outside the window of the cold south-facing room. At the mercy of my hunger, I decided to leave the office and venture to the local café around the corner where I was well acquainted with the owner, Ron.

The bustling main road hummed with life. Cars zoomed amongst the rustling of the trams that rattled up the tracks, chiming distinctively to alert pedestrians and motorists to their presence. The red man on the pedestrian lights ordered me to wait until I could cross the road, as I basked in the un-seasonally warm sun and fresh air, before the friendlier green man appeared, accompanied with his shrill sound, to signify that it was safe to egress. As I opened the door to the café, the smell of roasted coffee beans and baked goods hit me like a pleasurable slap to the face, along with the distinct sound of the coffee machine and lively chatter. I was greeted by the cheery smile of Ron from behind the counter, a friendly-faced, middle-aged man with glasses and short dark hair.

'Jack! How you going, mate?'

'Ronny, I'm good, mate. How are you?'

'Not bad, mate. You know how it is.'

'How's business?'

'Not too bad. As you can see, we're pretty chockers in here, so why don't you sit outside and I'll bring you some lunch and we'll have a chat.'

'Awesome, give me a coffee and one of those paninis and I'll see you out there.'

'Of course, mate, coming right up. Have a seat.'

I left the busy coffee shop and pulled up a chair with a scrape along the pavement, nestling amongst other patrons who sat on the footpath of the busy street, happily enduring the sunshine. People scurried about to complete their various errands and moved about the bundle of shops diligently, which mixed with the outside clamour to form a certain urban ambience. I started to read the paper that I had acquired from inside when my items were brought to me by Ron, who placed them on the table and took a seat across from me.

'Ah, bugger, mate, I need a rest. My missus might go crook at me but all good, I'm old.'

'You've earnt it. You're always flat knacker in there.'

'Most of the time, yeah. Sometimes it feels like every man and his dog wants a bloody coffee!'

'I'm sure it does, although I'm sure you guys do pretty well here. It's a busy little business.'

'Yeah, it's decent, Jack, but the bloody landlord is a greedy bastard. Charges us a bloody arm and a leg for rent and ups it every chance he gets!'

'Bugger.'

'Yeah, look, I could talk about my disdain for him until the cows come home, but anyway, how about those Lions? I watched it Sunday, thought of you. They looked real good.'

'My word, they did. Exciting times. Your blokes, not so much.'

'Oh, Jack, don't get me started, mate. The players run around like bloody headless chooks!'

'Yeah, might be a bit of pain to come, Ronny.'

'I reckon. Anyway, how's business for you?'

'Been pretty good. I'm actually doing a huge reno at Rocco Falcone's house.'

'Fair dinkum, the bloody mafioso?'

'Yeah, mate, him. He's a prick.'

'You know, I've never heard a good word spoken about that bloke. What's he been like?'

'I think you can guess exactly what he's been like.'

'Ah, those blokes are honestly just a different breed. I know his mate, Tony Antonello.'

'You're kidding?'

'Nah, how come?'

'He just rang me and invited me to dinner for a business meeting. He wants me to do some work for him. How do you know him?'

'In the way wogs know wogs. Our parents are from the same region in Italy.'

'What's he like?'

'He's actually a decent bloke on face value, quite charming. But I wouldn't trust him as far as I could kick him on a personal level. In saying that, professionally, I don't know. He must be good. I mean, his developments are top notch and he's never had any trouble from his actual building projects. It's just other stuff.'

'Righto, well, I s'pose at the very least, I'll get a decent feed.'

'Oh, mate, grouse food. But you know what Truffatore means?'

'No clue.'

'Crook.'

'Like criminal?'

'Yep. Cheeky bugger he is. Anyway, I better get inside before I get my head bitten off. Enjoy your lunch and good luck tonight.'

'Thanks heaps. See you, mate.'

After a decent read of the paper and something to eat, I returned to the office to tie up some loose ends before heading home early to enjoy the sunny afternoon with the girls. As I pulled up out the front, I stepped out of the car and studied the house in all of its glorious deficiencies, my mind wandering as to where the money would go if I accepted the anticipatedly lucrative job with Tony. The blistered weatherboards needed painting, the warped veranda deck needed replacement and the front garden deserved some beautification, to name a few things that I could immediately pick out. As I entered the house, I ventured down the short, cream-coloured hallway, my feet lightly tapping on the conduit Persian rug that led to the open doorway of the lounge. The living area was unpopulated; its dark leather couch had its back to me and faced the television that lay under the window. A black metal fireplace sat next to it, adorned in an enchanting dark red and green tiling pattern at its base; it was a feature that I deemed worthy of restoration should we inherit more money. The cream tone enveloped the walls of the room and stretched to the old kitchen that formed a U-shape in the far corner, its orange timber cupboards and dark vinyl benchtops in dire need of replacement. Open windows along the back wall allowed a light to shine in from the backyard that made the corkboard floor glisten, bringing with it the sweet resonations of the girls outside. I walked towards the back door and out onto the shoddy decking, which revealed the rippled underbelly of timber that was pinned to the bearers upside-down. The sound of a distant lawn mower roared, along with the squawk of crows and the kinder chirps of smaller birds. Resplendent sunshine drenched the tired backyard. Helena stood at the clothesline at the end of a bricked path, which sat in the middle of the backyard amongst a sea of weeded grass. A solitary lemon tree grew in the back corner, opposite a miserable tin shed, which provided some shade for Matilda who crawled gleefully on the lawn.

'Hello!' I greeted them as Helena turned her head from the washing line.

'Hey, high flyer!' Helena joked as I pecked her lips.

'And what about you, little grub?' I said as I moved to the grass to cuddle Matilda, who appeared to be exalted by my presence.

I took a seat on the scratchy lawn and Matilda nestled into my lap, her cheeks a little flushed and her body warmed by the heat of the sun. I swatted away some of the flies that buzzed about both of our faces.

'Luce was happy to mind her?'

'Absolutely rapt.'

'Great. I'm a little bit nervous about it, actually.'

'How come?'

'I dunno, could be a big moment for the business and my career. He sounded pretty intimidating on the phone, sort of a commanding voice.'

'You reckon they'll make you bury bodies under the houses or something?'

I laughed as Helena shot me a cheeky look.

'Maybe you'll be able to charm Tony and get us more money.'

'I was thinking that or a low-cut dress?'

'I need his eyes focused on me!'

'Well, just give me the signal if things aren't going well and I'll put out, alright?'

'I wouldn't want to punish him.'

'Well, guess who just talked themselves out of sex for a while?'

We chuckled as I let Tilly crawl around on the grass again.

'It would be really nice to get this place up to scratch if I do take the job. This tired old backyard needs a makeover. It would be nice to give her a place for swings and a cubby.'

'Yeah, I would love that. Depends how much the job is, I s'pose. I would love to gut that kitchen, fix the floor, paint the whole house. You know, the things we planned to have done by now when we bought it.'

'Hmm, yeah. Life got in the way, I s'pose. I tell you what, a dog would be nice too.'

'Yeah, you reckon Tilly would be good at feeding it and walking it? Maybe they can toilet train together?'

'Aren't you a comedian.'

'Maybe when she's a bit older. But seriously, I would love all of that. And at the end of the day, it's just a dinner and you can always so no. So, let's just enjoy it. We haven't been out anywhere nice for a while.'

I nodded as I turned to see Matilda attempting to eat a dandelion, which I quickly removed from her clutches to her evident dismay. Helena finished hanging the washing and moved over to us both before picking up Matilda with a groan.

'You're getting heavy, Tilly! I'm going to put her to sleep so she's not cranky for aunty Lucy.'

We spent the rest of the afternoon on the back veranda, both reading books and enjoying the change in seasonality. Matilda joined us after her nap and we watched the sun lower in the sky against its blue backdrop until it hung low enough in the west for us to relocate inside. Helena decided to start getting ready for dinner as I fed Matilda and waited for Lucy, who arrived at nightfall. After her entrance, I retired to the bedroom to get ready, opening the door and sliding in to find Helena standing in her underwear in front of the wardrobe, deliberating on her attire for the evening.

'What should I wear, Jack?'

'I'm just going to wear chinos and a shirt, so whatever the female equivalent is of that. Maybe a nice dress, like you would wear if we were going on a date night.'

'It's a fancy restaurant, though.'

'I'm sure you'll look beautiful in anything, Helena.'

'Thanks, but I think after this deal you need to take your wife shopping for some new clothes.'

'Yes, boss.'

I kissed her on the cheek as I removed my clothes and moved into the little ensuite to shower. When I returned to the bedroom, I found that she had decided on a simple black dress that hugged her hips so wonderfully well. She looked beautiful, her hair was worn up, earrings flickered from her ears, with a face that gleamed intricately with an enhanced made-up splendour. She sat on the bed, applying the finishing touches, with the sound of soft music playing from a speaker that we had on the bedside.

'Well, don't you scrub up a treat, my love,' I said, cloaked in my towel as I moved to the wardrobe to reveal my garment choices for the occasion.

'Thank you, babe. So nice to get dressed up a bit.'

'I'll just get dressed and we'll organise a cab.'

'Cab? I presumed I would just drive.'

'No, no, Mummy and Daddy are getting pissed tonight, I reckon.'

'I suppose he'll probably order us some nice wine.'

'I bloody hope so.'

I dressed in some light chinos and a black shirt before sitting on the bed to put my boots on. It was then that *Secret Garden* began its melodic hypnosis as it resounded from the music player.

I turned to Helena; she flashed a gentle smile that she seemed to save for moments like these as I reached out my hand to find hers, with our eyes meeting tenderly.

I was transported back to our wedding day every time that I heard it; I could remember drawing her in as we began to sway and become lost in the music. I could feel the silkiness of her wedding dress as I caressed her hips and small of her back. I could smell the bouquet of her subtle perfume; she felt so small in my arms. I could see the faces of family and friends whirl around as we danced, aware that everyone was watching but feeling like we were the only two in the room. I could remember staring into her eyes and seeing the future; not being one bit scared, but rather so excited at what our life together could be. I had never existed in a moment so loving; it was like falling in love all over again. As we broke from our momentary solace, I kissed her soft lips with a wordless affection. No words were needed.

Chapter 9
Truffatore

The cab rolled through the busy street that the restaurant was situated on, with crowds of people dining al fresco outside of Italian restaurants that greeted us with exotic sounding names. I nervously sat in the front of the cab next to our driver, with Helena in the back, as we pulled up out the front of the restaurant and I paid him for his fare.

'Nervous?' Helena asked as we walked past the hordes out the front of the restaurant who were sat on tables or queued on the footpath to wait for one.

'A bit. Still not sure why.'

'It's because it means something to you. But don't worry, you'll kill it. You're one of the best.'

I glanced at her appreciatively as I opened the door and let her in the restaurant before me. The intimately lit restaurant was busy, the sound of a heaving kitchen resonated from the back of the room and wound its way amongst the comfortable gaiety of the diners. The space was a mixture of dark tables and opaque floorboards; the walls were decorated with black and white photographs of Italian effects, which oozed a certain nostalgic charm and nestled in with the smell of yeast and garlic that perfumed the air.

'Good evening, how may I help you?' a waiter asked at the entrance, dressed neatly in a white shirt and black vest with bow tie, complete with an Italian accent.

'My wife and I have a reservation with Tony.'

'Ah, right. Mr and Mrs Newton?'

'That's us.'

'Great, come with me.'

He led us to a stairwell that spiralled in the back corner, taking us past an opening that looked directly into the kitchen, with sweaty chefs dressed in white, who scurried about in organised chaos to feed the awaiting patrons. We journeyed up the stairs that snaked around into a second level, joining another pundit of happy customers, as we were led into a small nook away from the crowd. A man, who I immediately recognised, stood up from the small table that he was seated at. He was an unexpectedly kind-faced man of average physique, with short dark hair and a black moustache that overhung small gapped teeth.

'Jack!' he cried as we both entered.

'Tony. Nice to meet you, mate,' I said as I shook his hand that returned a firm grip before turning to Helena who stood behind me. 'This is my wife, Helena.'

'Oh, aren't you an absolute vision,' he said as he kissed the back of her hand politely. 'Please, sit.'

We took our seats at the table, which was adorned with wine glasses and a small candle that added to the cosily dim lighting of the windowless room. Tony spoke to his waiter who was hovering nearby.

'Angelo, vino, per favore.'

The waiter nodded his head and left the room as Tony re-joined his seat across from us.

'How are you both? So lovely to meet you.' He smiled.

'Great,' said Helena.

'Fantastic,' I added.

'Are you both red wine drinkers?'

We nodded together happily.

'Brilliant, I've got a real nice bottle coming for us. Also, any dietary requirements? Or things you hate?'

'Jack will eat just about anything!' Helena joked. 'And I'm not fussy, especially with anything Italian.'

'She was a vegetarian when I first met her,' I informed. 'I made her see the light, thankfully.'

'Well, that's good news.' Tony assuredly laughed. 'Because the chef is cooking us something special.'

The waiter returned with a bottle of red wine and proceeded to pour some for us both to taste, as was the custom. We both sipped it and nodded affirmatively before he filled all of our glasses.

'I get that from my parents' home town. Bloody expensive but nice to have on special occasions with good company,' Tony advised. 'Well, here's to a happy life, full of good food and wine.'

He held up the crimson-filled glass as we copied the gesture before clinking our glasses and having a mouthful.

'Lovely,' Helena remarked. 'Where are your family from in Italy, Mr Antonello?'

'Helena, please call me Tony,' he charmingly added. 'They're from a small town in the north of Italy, between Milan and Venice, a beautiful place. Have you been to anywhere in Italy?'

'We both have been to Italy and all around Europe,' Helena answered. 'Just magical, some of those places.'

'I've done a few backpacking trips around,' I informed.

'Europeans have just got it right, I think,' Tony began. 'They have a greater quality of life, whereas in Australia, we have a better standard of living but sometimes we prioritise the wrong things. An Italian will take time to enjoy a great meal and a siesta after. Don't get me wrong, they work bloody hard, but they also take time to smell the roses more than we do here.'

'Agreed,' I concurred. 'It would be a great way of life. Although, I feel like after having our daughter, we appreciate the little things more. Don't you think, Helena?'

'Yeah, definitely,' Helena said. 'Life is slower but a happy slow.'

'What's her name?' Tony asked.

'Matilda,' Helena replied.

'I'm sure she is beautiful,' Tony said.

The waiter brought over three bowls that he carefully balanced on his hands and forearm, placing them at the table as we curiously viewed the pasta dishes, which exuded a deliciously strong smell of truffle and garlic.

'This is a handmade ravioli with a creamy truffle, white wine and garlic sauce. Trust me, it is just divine,' Tony informed.

As we all tucked into the dish, I couldn't help but be quite astounded by how charming and likeable the man across from me was. He flashed his kind face as we ate, he listened intently as we talked, and his intimidating phone voice was softer and congenial. I still trod alongside a mild hesitance, with Ron's words ringing in my ears, aware that this could all have been a carefully contrived facade. However, I felt my walls come down as I began to like the man who I had only known and judged through the eyes of the media.

I studied him as we ate. His dark, lightly salted hair was minutely thinning on top, exacerbated by a small widow's peak; his dense moustache seemed to merge with his nose hair ever so slightly. He flashed small, rounded teeth whenever he smiled, which looked like a crooked off-white picket fence amongst a hedge line. As the entrees were taken away, he began the business talk.

'Okay, well let's get down to brass tax, shall we? Before the wine does the talking for us! Now, Jack, as I said to you on the phone, Rocco recommended your company. I know your partner has had issues with him, but he really respects your designs. I've seen the plans for his renovation and they were impressive. Your attention to detail is something I admire. I've been to look at a few of the projects you've undertaken and I loved them all. I want for my next project to ooze the care and sophistication that your designs have. They seem to have a certain charm.'

'Thank you, Tony,' Helena squeezed my leg admiringly, taking a nip of her wine.

'I suppose to get a wife as wonderful as yours, you must be charming. Hey, Jack?'

'That or dumb luck,' I joked.

'He can be charming when he wants to be.' Helena sparkled with a rosy red-wine glow to complement her rouged lips that stained the rim of her glass.

'How big is the project?' I asked.

'Bloody massive. Do you know the old Bond Paper Factory?'

'Yeah, I do.'

'Well, I bought it. I figure that massive brick factory in the middle could be an apartment block and then around it I want townhouses. But, Jack, my developments are functional and practical. I like them to have character and not be the cheap as chips, money-making bullshit that other developers do. What do you think?'

'That's pretty much exactly what I'm about.'

'I knew you were the right man for the job. But I have a few requirements of you.'

'What would they be exactly?'

'Well, as I told you on the phone, I've dealt with bigger firms before and they give you the run around. Can't get a hold of who you need when you want. You know how it is, I'm sure.'

'Yeah, I worked for one of them a few years back. Hated it.'

'Well, after my last project, I'd had enough and thought next time, I'm going to try someone smaller. Someone who will answer my calls when I need them to, but most importantly, who cares about their design and is invested in the project. Rocco tells me you are that kind of bloke.'

'I'd like to think so.'

It was at that moment that the waiter re-emerged with several new dishes and placed them at the table with us again peering intently at them.

'Alright, we've got lobster with garlic butter sauce and these here are mushrooms with mascarpone and parmesan. Trust me, they are unbelievable.'

'Oh, Tony, thank you so much. This looks incredible!' Helena exclaimed.

'More wine?' he asked.

'Sure, why not?' Helena giggled, possibly already a little tipsy.

'That's the spirit,' Tony snickered. 'Un'altra bottiglia, Angelo.'

'Certo, Tony,' the server responded with a nod as he left the room.

We tucked into the food with groans of delight, with Tony advising us that we would reconvene the business chat after dinner, as he wanted us to enjoy the food and appreciate the moment. It was another endearing move on his part.

'Alright, so back to the nitty gritty,' Tony recommenced as the plates were cleared and we sat with contented bellies. 'If we're going to enter into this working relationship, I should outline my number one stipulation. I need your company and all of its attention for the entire build.'

'What do you mean by our full attention, exactly?'

'I mean, I am your only project for the entire time it runs.'

'Oh, wow. Right.'

'And this is my offer. I feel like the project will be at least twelve months, so you will show me your books for the last financial year and I will pay you the amount your business made plus twenty per cent. But not only that, Jack and Helena, this relationship could help set you up for the future. I am a very well-connected man. I have pull in top schools around the city, for instance, so I'm a good man to have on your side with a little one that you want the best for,' he said confidently as he shifted back in his chair a little nonchalantly as if to relax the conversation.

'Well, yes, I could imagine there would be many perks,' I responded.

'That's just the beginning. Are you a footy fan, Jack?'

'Yeah, love it.'

'Well, I have a corporate box at the MCG and Docklands, which is yours whenever you want it. You work with me, I give you a company car with a petrol card for the year, even though you won't technically be an employee of mine. For your little girl, we start a university fund, which I invest with my brokers and by the time she's eighteen, she can pay her uni fees in full. And you, Helena, what are your plans? What would be a dream career for you?'

'Well, I was a physio. I mean, still technically am, so I'd like to go back to work one day and have my own clinic, I suppose.'

'Perfect. Well, one of my developments, I build a little shop and we start a business for you.'

'My gosh, that all sounds so wonderful,' Helena stated dreamily.

'Now, Jack, for you I have big plans. I have influence with the Architecture Council. There are awards that I could get you nominated for. If you win, well, from there you could become one of Australia's best architects. This could be a springboard for your career.'

'It's a lot to take in,' I answered with mild astonishment.

'I'll leave you two to discuss, but these are just some gifts from me if you both decide to agree. I'll be back in a bit.'

With that, he produced a small black cardboard bag with a fancy roped handle from beside him. He placed it on the table before rising from his chair and politely bowing his head at us as he left. I turned to Helena, who appeared excitedly surprised as she curiously gazed at the bag.

'What do you think is in there?' she asked.

'Before I look, what do you think about it all?' I whispered.

'My god, all of that sounds unbelievable. Like I'm kind of shocked at how amazing and generous that sounds,' she tipsily exclaimed.

'You a bit pissed?' I sniggered.

'A bit.' She smirked drunkenly. 'But I am so surprised by how un-Rocco-like he is.'

'I thought you were.' I laughed. 'Yeah, me too. He seems like a nice bloke but we still need to remember what we've heard of him. He's not exactly law abiding in everything that he does.'

'But, Jacko, I read about him today. None of his run-ins have had anything to do with building. Mainly tax stuff. Pretty tame, really. Nothing violent. I'm sure he's not exactly an angel but this seems like such a good opportunity. I mean, you don't have to worry about getting work for a whole year and you'll earn more than you did. This could be a springboard like he said. He seems to appreciate building and could talk about architecture until the cows come home, just like you. And think of all those perks that he just mentioned, it could be the greatest opportunity that will set us up for life.'

'Yeah, look, I'm leaning the same way. I'm wary this could all be a front to pull the wool over our eyes but I'm happy to entertain the idea. I'll talk it over with George and see what he reckons. I mean, Tony is still closely associated with Rocco at the end of the day. And I know he hasn't been convicted of anything too serious, but where there's smoke there's fire, don't forget.'

'I understand. But they're not exactly going to make you be their hitman or drug runner now, are they? You'll just be doing developments for a client as you usually do, but on a bigger scale. Much of a muchness, really.'

'But do I want to be doing business with this calibre of people?'

'I know. But on the other hand, do you want to pass up an amazing opportunity by overthinking it?'

'Yeah, good point. Food for thought.'

'I think you're a naturally cautious person but think of all the possibilities. Your business will expand dramatically. Matilda can go to a good school; we can renovate the house and not have any financial stress. That would be the best feeling and the most wonderful gift for all of us. Especially if we want to have another kid.'

'Yeah, I know. Lots to think about.'

'Jack, I'll respect whatever decision you make, and I want you to be a hundred per cent comfortable with it. The life you provide us is wonderful and we will live a fabulous life either way. So, let's just enjoy ourselves and worry about the harder decisions later.'

'Thank you, my love.'

I kissed her red wine lips as she smiled contentedly.

'I wonder what's in this?' I said as I picked up the bag that had a bit of weight behind it.

'Have a look!'

I brought it closer to look inside; there were two small packages in it that I removed. I opened the first one, a bulky leather box, to reveal a strikingly lavish wristwatch. I exchanged a stunned look with Helena. The other package, a thinner velvet box, revealed a diamond necklace that sparkled glamorously despite the dimmed light as Helena's face lit up with shock.

'Oh my god,' Helena murmured.

'We can't accept these,' I stammered.

'It's a lot. I don't know what to say.'

Shortly after, Tony re-entered with the waiter and presented us with small dessert bowls of tiramisu.

'A little treat for us all,' he said as he sat back in his seat, gathering the bag off the table with a poised grin. 'I trust you liked what you saw?'

'Tony, I want to thank you for your generosity,' I began as we ate our desserts.

'Yes, me too,' Helena agreed.

'You're both very welcome,' he replied.

'Obviously, I have to talk to my business partner about it all.'

'Naturally. Talk things over with him and then get back to me in the next couple of weeks or so.'

'Great. I would appreciate that.'

'Now, let's just enjoy the dessert.'

'It's amazing,' Helena remarked. 'I can never get mine to taste anywhere near as good as this.'

'Our chef is one of the best,' Tony bragged.

We chatted happily for a little while longer before we finished our desserts and bottle of wine and amicably parted company with Tony. As we drove home in the cab, down the dark and quiet streets, Helena nodded off and dozed on my shoulder. I didn't feel one ounce of tiredness; I was joyfully floating, not only from the merry glow of alcohol but also from the awe-inspiring disbelief and gratitude at how fortunate my life was. Yes, I was still wary, but I was unable to contain the optimism that I felt towards the unbelievable opportunity that had just presented itself. In all honestly, I felt like life was nearing an excellence that I never thought possible.

Chapter 10
Good Help Is so Hard to Find

I found myself at the office toiling away the next day, once again basking in the simple joy of working solo and content with a sense of space and freedom. The pleasant resonance of indie music filled the air as I sat at Elaine's usual domicile of production for the day. Not only was there more available natural light at the front desk but it also afforded me with the ability to answer phones or deal with anyone that decided to grace me with their presence through the front door. Midway through the day, the shrill of the phone broke the musical tranquillity of the office with its obnoxious shriek, causing me to begrudgingly pause the song and pick it up.

'New Fullarton Builds,' I answered.

'Jacko, is that you?' a familiar voice asked. 'It's Ted.'

'Yeah, Teddy it's me. How you going, mate?'

'I'm alright, thanks, mate. I'm just having a bit of an issue with the bank today and that cheque Georgey gave me on Friday.'

'Oh right, what's the problem?'

'Well, I cashed the cheque and my bank just rang me to let me know that it bounced. I've tried to get onto Georgey but there's no answer and he hasn't replied to any of my messages.'

'Spewing. That's no good at all, mate! Yeah, look, I have no clue about the financial stuff, unfortunately. I gave it up when Helena was pregnant and Elaine took it all over.'

'Yeah, I knew that. Do you reckon you could chase it up for me and sort it out?'

'Oh, yes. Of course, mate. I'll try and get onto George or Elaine too and then if I can't, I'll chase it up with the bank. There must be a mistake of some sort.'

'Thanks, Jacko. It's just that it's a shitload of cash too. I need to pay my boys and all the bills, you know?'

'Yeah, Teddy, I get it. Leave it with me, okay?'

Ted thanked me and ended the call. I put the phone down and leant back in my chair to ponder for a second on what the issue could be, a little frustrated with the fact that I would be distracted from the mountain of work that I had to complete. I decided that my first port of call would be to try to make contact with Elaine and George myself, but after attempting numerous calls to no avail, I resolved in sending them both a text message to request that they contact me. Next, I set about to examine all of the banking for myself; after all, I knew all of the passwords to our accounts. So, I opened up a new window on the laptop and procured the internet banking website, typing in the account number and password with a furious mashing of keys that broke the noiselessness of the office. However, after a few failed attempts, I was informed that the details were incorrect. I gazed at the screen, flummoxed and furrow-browed, questioning how this could be.

I picked up the phone and dialled the number that it advised me to call on the screen, and after following the prompts, I got onto an operator. In an Indian accent, he requested my account name and number, which I gave him, before asking for an internet banking password. Unfortunately, I was not privy to it. In fact, I had never implemented one when I had performed the accounting duties; for some reason, it had seemingly been instigated by Elaine. The beginnings of concern began to swirl as the man on the end of the line informed me to visit the bank branch in person and we terminated our phone call.

I promptly closed my laptop and moved to the front door of the office to lock it, struggling to comprehend the reasons for these errors and puzzled as to why convoluted alterations had been put in place. I made my way down the corridor with the soles of my leather shoes thudding on the vinyl floorboards as they echoed around the silent space. The back door was locked with a jangling of keys and a heavy thud as I left the building and hopped in my car.

I was perplexed by the dubious issue that had presented itself and filled with mild anxiety of the unknown as my brain began to catastrophise and provide me with the most irreverent solutions. I trusted Elaine and George and didn't believe that they would have done anything sinister but I was still plagued with an anxious agitation. Luckily, one of my best friends, Royce Downs, was the manager of the branch and would be able to provide me with answers to my current distress.

My cognisance was hindered for the whole car ride, with a form of human auto-pilot taking over to commandeer the vehicle whilst my mind was busy running an inner monologue. In my next moment of presence, I had arrived at the bank branch, burdened with heavy thought.

I parked the car and made my way inside with a slam of the door.

'Good afternoon, sir. How can I help you?' the woman who greeted me at the front desk of the bank asked, dressed smartly in a dark pantsuit with a friendly guise adorning her face.

'I need to speak to Royce,' I replied. 'I'm having an issue with my account.'

'Of course. I'll get him for you. Please, take a seat,' she informed, gesturing me to a chair situated near the desk. 'What's your name?'

'Jack Newton. I'm a mate of his,' I answered as I took up her offer.

I felt a little clammy. My legs jittered, much like an uneasy child awaiting their engagement outside the principal's office. The chair began to feel uncomfortable as I became mildly agitated by the quiet environment of the bank and the fact that time seemed to crawl at an agonising pace. I intently watched the woman as she knocked on Royce's door and informed him that he had someone waiting to see him, before returning to notify me that he would be with me momentarily. She took her place back behind the front desk and shortly after, the office door opened, and Royce emerged from behind it to make his way over to me. As he walked, his stoutly kind face smiled with his slightly rotund build, complemented by his mildly receding, short brown hair that was always pristine and fitted with a chic, neatly fashioned hairstyle. When not localised in a professional setting, he could be quite witty and was gifted with a phenomenal ability to do the most amazing impersonations. However, on this occasion, I was most likely to experience his dry, humourless, professional persona as he greeted me with a handshake.

'G'day, Jacko. Good to see you, mate,' he said as he manually indicated that we should relocate to his office. 'Come in.'

I followed him to his office door where he gestured for me to enter first and closed the door behind us as we both sat at his small desk that was scattered with various documents, along with a computer and phone.

'How's things?' he enquired informally as he sat back in his chair and clasped his hands, resting them on his stomach.

'I'm not sure, Roycey,' I responded uneasily. 'You know Teddy Worsopp?'

Royce nodded in affirmation.

'Well, he rang me today and told me a cheque we gave him bounced. I tried to log onto the internet banking and even rang the call centre but Elaine has put all these new passwords on the account so I can't access anything. I'm getting a little nervous here, mate, I just need to know what's going on with the business account and why the cheque bounced.'

'Righto, let's have a squizz,' he said as he turned to his computer and began typing away feverishly with a solemnly squinted look on his face, before reaching for his glasses and putting them on, which remedied the narrow-eyed aspect of his countenance.

After a moment, Royce looked up at me from his computer with a blank stare, hesitating before he spoke.

'There's no money in the account, Jacko. That's why the cheque bounced.'

An icily cold perspiration began to run down my back as my body temperature rose with a mild panic that set in.

'How... how is that possible?' I stammered, gawking at him in astonishment.

'Well,' Royce began and then paused as he scrolled down with his computer mouse to study the transaction history. 'It appears that the funds from the business account have been transferred into another account. This has been going on for at least twelve months. More than that, actually, probably eighteen. Small amounts at first but then building up to a massive amount a couple of days ago.'

'My god!' I cried in shock. 'That was the time when Elaine took over the accounts!'

We both sat silently to drink in the gravity of the situation, my blood pressure rising as I tried to comprehend all that was happening.

'So, you're saying you had no knowledge of this at all?' Royce questioned.

'Of course not, mate! None at all!' I replied in panic.

Royce hesitated with a stunned look on his face.

'So, just to clarify, we're talking possible embezzlement here?' he quizzed.

I took a deep breath and exhaled, gazing up at him in genuine disbelief.

'I think so. I just can't believe they would do this. Whose account has the money been transferred to?'

Royce paused for a moment as he ogled his computer screen for an extended period, making various clicks of his mouse that ricocheted through the silently tense air.

'Elaine and George's personal account,' he uttered as he looked at me in horror.

I froze, as I felt the colour drain from my face, the stark realisation jolting me from any form of incredulity. Royce's eyes flickered as if his brain was hurriedly rummaging for words to fill the moment but couldn't, as we both sat for an instant in a complete hush. We both seemed to struggle with the fact that Elaine and George were capable of an unfavourable undertaking such as this; Royce was acquainted with them too and looked on them with the mutual praise that I had.

'Okay, mate, I'm gonna have to call the police,' he announced with hesitation as he broke the silence by promptly picking up the phone that sat on his desk.

'Roycey, I need to get out of here,' I spluttered as I became increasingly distressed.

I felt myself grow lightheaded; my heart rate elevated and breathing became heavily laboured. Royce noticed and moved the receiver from his ear to rest it on his shoulder.

'Jack, go home,' he said firmly. 'I'll tell the detective to go to your place to find you.'

I rose from the chair immediately and left the office without a word, stumbling out of the branch and into my car in a daze. I sat there for a minute in awe; it was a pinch-yourself moment that almost didn't feel real. My mind raced along with a heart that pounded nervously in my chest. The heat of my body engulfed me, as a balmy perspiration gathered on my skin. My lungs felt like they were suddenly unable to capture any oxygen from the atmosphere. The car began to feel tiny and enclosed, like a cage to a hapless beast. I opened the car door and desperately gulped for air. After taking a moment, I fumbled with my keys and shakily jammed them into the ignition to start the car. I drove off, journeying home with my mind occupied with millions of comings and goings, as if the neurons in my brain were launching messages with the seeming veracity of machine gun fire.

Chapter 11
You Are a Tourist in Your Own Life

The car hummed along with the sound of rubber tyres over bitumen as it broke the air during the drive home. I valiantly fought the tears that gathered in my eyes, which made my vision blurry at times and tickled my cheeks as they ran down my face and leapt onto my lap. When I came to a halt out the front of my house, my emotions gushed from me like the breach of a dam wall. I started to bawl in the face of the overwhelming situation. With the melancholy came anger, driving me to slam my fists onto the steering wheel repeatedly and scream in a primal reaction; the disbelief and shock had seemingly undergone a metamorphosis into fury.

I sat in my car for a long while, not wanting to get out, as I stared into the distance and attempted to gain some mental composure. A wind gusted from the cloudy sky and billowed leaves around the quiet street. I looked in the rear vision mirror and wiped my face of tears. My eyes were glassily crimson and pained. As soon as she saw me, Helena would know that something had gone awry; crying, or indeed any extrinsic outpouring of emotion, wasn't exactly a common occurrence of mine. Despite the horrid circumstances though, Helena would be a calming influence like she always was – grace and serenity personified in both voice and disposition. I left the car with a loud exhale and made my way into our house, walking down the corridor in a voyage that seemed to take place in a slow-motion weightlessness. I entered the living room to the sweet smell of cinnamon and vanilla and found Helena baking in the kitchen of the quiet house, shadowed by a murky light that penetrated the back window. Matilda was nowhere to be seen and I gathered by the quietude of the place that she was sleeping.

'Hello,' she turned and whispered with a smile, vindicating my inference, as I made my way towards her without a response to her statement.

She twisted and looked at me again, the smile on her face fading into concern as she quickly broke from what she was doing and moved to meet me. I fell into her arms and we stood there for a moment, enveloped within each other as I began to weep.

'Babe, what's wrong?' Helena uttered nervously before she leaned out of our embrace and placed both of her hands on my shoulders. She stared into my eyes, an increased uneasiness displayed on her face.

'Let's go out the back and talk,' I replied meekly, taking her hand and leading her out the back door onto the veranda.

We sat on the outdoor chairs of the covered back deck, in view of the overcast sky and neat, west-facing backyard. Helena's concerned face glared at me. I sighed, pausing on how to inform her of the events that had occurred.

'Jack,' she said despairingly as she placed a hand on my thigh. 'What is it?'

I once again sighed as I formulated a response.

'Well,' I began nervously with a quivering voice. 'Today I got a call from Ted, who told me that a cheque that George gave him from us had bounced. So, I tried to look at the account online and then rang the call centre but Elaine had changed all the passwords. Anyway, I went to the bank and spoke to Royce, he looked up the account and we found that there are no funds in the account because Elaine and George have transferred it all into their personal account.'

I paused as I began to tremble with a despaired anger.

'They've been doing it since she took over the accounting. It seems like they've stolen everything from us and done a runner.'

Helena's eyes and mouth had widened as she stared fearfully, searching for words.

'They've been embezzling money?' she finally uttered.

'It seems that way,' I answered despondently.

She turned away and stared blankly in distress, her eyes aflicker in an attempt to take in all that she had heard as we sat for a moment in silence.

'I am absolutely shocked,' she eventually stammered, continuing her vacant gaze into nothingness.

'Me too,' I whispered as I clutched her hand and squeezed it.

After a long pause, she appeared to snap out of her daze and turned to me with regained composure.

'My god, Jack, are you alright?' she asked, returning the squeeze of my hand with the sudden realisation that the empire in which I had prided myself was crumbling.

'I'm just devastated,' I replied. 'I'm in complete and utter shock. I can't believe they would do this to us, you know. I mean, they've left us with nothing – we have no money. Essentially, we're bankrupt. It makes me so angry.'

We stared at each other, both with apprehension written all over our faces, our minds tormented with the abrupt revelation of our life being spun upside down. Helena shook her head as tears welled in her eyes, while mine began to empathise and gain some as well.

'Well, whatever happens,' she started falteringly, tears rolling down her cheeks. 'We'll get through it together. We have a little bit of savings and Mum and Dad will help us if need be.'

I nodded in agreeance as we embraced upon the release of the proverbial emotional floodgates and wept together for a minute.

'So, what do we do now?' Helena snivelled as we ended our grip on each other and wiped our teary faces.

'Royce told me that the police will come here apparently,' I informed, 'and we'll go from there, I s'pose.'

'We need to catch these bastards!' Helena remarked with an angry sniffle.

A frosty breeze blew through the backyard as we sat there for what seemed like a while, clouded by a storm of uncertainty. Helena nestled into the side of my neck and I put my arm around her; both our faces voided as our minds ticked over in contemplation, vexed with a mixture of anger and panic. Eventually, the silence was broken by Matilda's cry that could be heard from the baby monitor in the kitchen, prompting us to get up and make our way into her room. She was upstanding in her cot when we opened the door and turned on the light, surrounded by the neutrally yellow walls that were decorated with various colourful pictures. Her face lit up with our entrance as Helena picked her up, kissing her head with an attempted brave face.

'Hello, Tilly!' she soothed. 'How was your sleep?

Helena handed Matilda to me and I swirled her around.

'Hello, little grub!' I cried excitedly, kissing her chubby cheeks. 'I missed you!'

Suddenly, there was a firm knock at the door that pierced the brief moment of ignorant joy and brought us back to a stark reality. I returned a knowing look with Helena, thinking that it would be the aforementioned detective, before handing Matilda back to her and moving to the covered window to peer through to the veranda. There stood an affable-looking man of similar age to me, with slick, dark brown hair, dressed commandingly in a dark suit, complete with a shirt and tie. I ventured from Matilda's room to open the door and was greeted by the man with a pleasant nod as he flashed his badge. To the side of his left eye, he had a small red scar that added to the confidently roguish charm that he appeared to exude. His front teeth were slightly discoloured, most likely appended from years of cigarette smoke or coffee drinking in response to the late nights and stresses of police work.

'Good evening, Mr Newton,' he stated authoritatively. 'My name is Detective Nicholas West. I was informed by the bank about the alleged embezzlement of funds from your company by your business partner.'

'Of course, come in,' I replied as I led him down the hallway and into the living room where we both sat down at the kitchen table.

Helena then emerged with Matilda in her arms and greeted the detective.

'This is my wife, Helena, and our baby, Matilda,' I explained as the detective acknowledged them congenially.

'Can I get you a coffee, Detective?' Helena asked as she placed Matilda down on the lounge floor to play and made her way into the kitchen to turn the kettle on.

'No, I'm fine, thank you,' he returned.

'Jack, I'm going to have one. Do you want one?' she enquired.

'Yes, please.' I nodded.

Helena removed cups from the cupboard. The detective and I watched Matilda with restrained smiles on our faces for a moment before he cleared his throat to begin formal proceedings.

'So, I have been filled in on the situation partially by a Mr Royce Downs, the bank manager you visited this afternoon. Let's just start by you telling me everything that occurred today in your words.'

'Well,' I began nervously as I cleared my throat just as the detective had done. 'I got a call today from one of our chippies that we use, who told me that a cheque George had given him had bounced.'

'And what would this man's name be?' Detective West interrupted as he began jotting on his notepad that he removed from his jacket pocket.

'Ted Worsopp.'

'Could you spell that for me?'

'W-O-R-S-O-P-P.'

The detective nodded and gestured for me to continue.

'So, after that I tried to find out what the issue was but couldn't get into the accounts online or on the phone because there were new passwords on them that prevented me from doing so.'

'And, who is in charge of all these accounts and their passwords?' the detective again interrupted as he paused from his note taking and looked up at me.

'My business partner's wife, Elaine. She took over the accounts stuff from me about eighteen months ago.'

'What are the full names of your business partner and his wife? And how do you know them both?'

'Their names are George and Elaine Fullarton, F-U-L-L-A-R-T-O-N. I met them both at the footy club, probably about five years ago.'

'And what is the name of the business that you all have?'

'New Fullarton Builds.'

'When was the last time that you saw or spoke to either of them?'

'Saw George last Friday on site of one of our jobs, which was actually when he gave the cheque to Ted. I saw Elaine later that same day at the office but the next day they left for a holiday to

Bali so I haven't seen them since. I tried calling them today but there was no answer.'

'Did they give you any details of their holiday? Hotel, flights, anything like that?'

'No, nothing.'

I paused for a moment on a sudden discovery as I glanced at the detective.

'Do you reckon it was all part of their plan? Take over the financial side of things, slowly siphon the money into their account and then take off?'

'It would appear to be a possibility at this stage. Did you ever suspect anything over the past eighteen months or so? There was no change in their behaviour or anything suspicious in nature?'

'Nah, nothing. But we have been so busy with the pregnancy and then Matilda so I have been fairly disconnected from the business side of things, to be honest.'

The detective nodded and then began to scribble away at his notepad once more. Helena brought over some coffee and placed a cup in front of me before sitting down next to me at the table.

'So, Detective,' Helena added after a momentary silence, 'what happens now?'

'Well, I will start my investigation immediately and see what I can find out,' the detective replied. 'I'm going to need all of their up-to-date contact information, phone numbers, emails, known addresses, names and contact details of all known family members and friends.'

With that, I retrieved my mobile phone from my pocket and proceeded to give the detective all of their known information. It was then that I grasped in astonishment, I didn't really know that much about them at all.

'That's all I really know. I know the suburb they lived in but I've never been to their house or even know their address. The business is registered here because I handled all the admin. They had no children and had never really mentioned any family. In fact, the only family member that I've ever heard George mention was his father, who I'm pretty sure lives in Port Moresby.'

'Is that Papua New Guinea?'

I nodded in affirmation at the detective's question.

'He was a navy man.'

'Do you know his name?'

'No idea.'

'Right, well, I should be able to find some info on all of them regardless,' he stated after he completed his scrawling. 'Do either of you have any further queries?'

Upon our denial, he reached into his jacket pocket and removed a business card, placing it in front of me on the table.

'Contact me if you think of anything or have any further questions, okay?'

We both nodded as he stood up from the table to shake our hands. Helena and I both thanked him as he collected his notepad and moved towards the front door in a heavy-footed gait with us in tow. We said our farewells as he departed from the house, before he stopped and turned back to look at us standing in the doorway from the path, reiterating that he would contact us promptly with his findings. The door was closed and we both made our way back to the table to sit and drink coffee with minimal words exchanged. The sound of the television voided the silence and entertained Matilda as we were engaged in a deep rumination that attempted to compute the day's revelations. Helena eventually left me with my thoughts to continue her baking, an activity that no longer represented the joy that it had a few hours ago but rather a mental distraction of sorts.

Later in the evening, I received a call that broke my zombie-like existence and interrupted the taciturnity of the room with the loud vibration of my mobile phone against the kitchen table. I moved over to pick it up and saw Ted's name flash up on the screen, which made me realise that I had completely forgotten to call him back.

'G'day, Teddy,' I stammered as I answered. 'I'm so sorry for not getting back to you, mate.'

'Everything alright?' he asked, appearing to appreciate the distress in my voice.

I took a deep breath and exhaled loudly.

'Look, Ted, I'm not sure how to tell you this. The reason the cheque bounced is because I've just found out that George and Elaine have been embezzling money from the company. They've stolen all the money we have and done a runner.'

Ted's gasp on the other line was audible.

'You're bloody kidding!'

'I wish I was.'

The line went quiet for a moment as it seemed Ted was lost for words. The silence was eventually broken with a sigh from him.

'I can't believe this. Georgey was always such a nice bloke!'

'I know, mate, I can't believe it either. I'm so sorry that you've copped it too. I promise, I had no idea what was going on.'

'Yeah, mate. I believe you, don't worry. Oh, Jacko, it's a shitload of money that I'm owed. This really hurts me. I don't know how I'm gonna pay my boys or my bills now.'

I had no words; I didn't know what to say. Ted swore loudly away from the phone and then moved it closer to his mouth again.

'Righto, mate, I'll let the other subbies know to stop work at the Falcone joint as well.'

'I'm so sorry, Teddy.'

'You didn't know, mate, it's okay. How are you doing with it all?'

'I'm shocked, mate. I'm bloody angry. I don't know what I'm going to do.'

'I'm so sorry this has happened to you and the girls, Jacko. Please let me know if you need anything from me, okay?'

'Thanks, legend.'

'Take care of yourself, mate. We'll be in touch.'

The phone call ended and I sat there with my head in my hands, my world unravelling through no fault of my own. I felt so powerless, so hopelessly feeble and out of control. It was then that I felt a warm embrace wrap me up from behind.

'We're in this together,' Helena whispered as she held me tight.

Matilda was the only one who really ate that night as neither of us could muster an appetite for anything in particular, with Helena's baked creation acting as our only form of nourishment. After we put Matilda down to sleep, both myself and Helena attempted to engage in slumber but soon realised that our tortured minds had other ideas and wanted to tick over in a heavy engagement. The night was incredibly restless as both of us drifted in between bouts of sleep amongst heavy hearts and minds.

IV.

A love so pure,

it calmed an anguished heart.

A love so bright,

we found each other in the dark.

Chapter 12
The Ice Is Getting Thinner

The sunlight greeted us both through gaps in the blinds of our bedroom window the next morning, signifying the completion of hours of tormented mental persecution under the cover of darkness. We both stared at one another, bleary-eyed for a few moments, exchanging looks of utter fatigue and worry that required no verbalisation. Our concentration was eventually broken by Matilda's cries. We both arose from bed wordlessly and rummaged for warmer clothing through stingingly tired vision, riddled with a debilitating fatigue that made my breath feel heavier than normal. The world seemed even bleaker than yesterday.

'I'll get her, you get the coffee,' Helena outlined as she left for Matilda's room.

I agreed to her demands and shuffled half-asleep into the living room towards the kitchen with a hazy head, squinting in the brighter luminescence. I switched on the kettle and grabbed the mugs from the cupboard, standing shakily to collect myself for a moment as the sound of the boiling kettle became more prominent in the still room. Helena emerged with Matilda and placed her in the high chair before I made my way over to greet her with a kiss and a cuddle that she delighted in. Helena busied herself by preparing her some breakfast. Eventually, after the kettle had finished its raucous task and coffees and breakfast were made, we both sat around the kitchen table mutely. Matilda messily ate away, while Helena and I sipped our cups of coffee in an endeavour to absorb a minute enhancement to our energy levels.

'Well, that was a shocker of a sleep, wasn't it?' Helena remarked with rhetoric as she held her coffee drowsily.

'I actually don't feel like I slept a wink,' I miserably replied, cautiously sipping on my hot coffee.

'Me either,' Helena responded. 'Reminds me of the days when she was first born.'

'True,' I muttered as I heard my phone ring and got up to get it from the kitchen counter.

The screen displayed a number that I wasn't familiar with as I received the call and greeted its occupant.

'Hello, Mr Newton, it's Detective West,' came the voice from down the line. 'My apologies if it's too early for you but I wanted to get to you first thing. How are you going?'

'Oh, mate, had better days,' I responded with a sigh. 'Didn't really get a wink last night. Just tossed and turned and couldn't switch my brain off.'

'Yes, to be expected, unfortunately,' he concurred. 'Look, I won't beat around the bush, my investigations have made some startling discoveries. May I come around as soon as possible?'

'Of course, mate,' I said.

'Okay, see you soon,' he responded as he ended the call.

I put the phone down on the kitchen bench and returned to the table.

'Was that the detective?' Helena quizzed.

'Yeah. He said he's made some startling discoveries.'

Helena's tired eyes widened a little as we sat in a lull and contemplated.

Within thirty minutes, there was a knock on the door that

made me break from watching Matilda play merrily. I marvelled at her ability to enjoy the simplest joys of life without having to worry about all of the sinister things that the world could offer. As I opened the front door, I was greeted by the stern-looking detective, who nodded at me as he entered before making his way to the kitchen table to sit in the same spot that he had during his previous visit. He then beckoned for us both to sit with him before waiting for us to join the table and begin with his news on the case.

'Okay, I'll get straight to it. I did some thorough research on Elaine and George Fullarton. It seems they had a lot of issues and a lot of problems that would cause them to do something like this and flee the country. They were gambling addicts who lost a lot of money. About twelve months ago, the bank foreclosed on their mortgage and they lost their house. They took to selling drugs and siphoning company money to try and make up for their gambling losses. They owe some bad people a lot of money.'

The detective paused as Helena and I glanced at each other in shock before looking back at the austere man in front of us. I searched for words but was unable to utter a sentence that conveyed the astonishment that I felt.

He continued after clearing his throat. 'Now, the money that they stole from the company was transferred into their personal account but now it has been transferred to an offshore account. This unfortunately means that we don't have the authority to freeze the funds, which is what we would normally do in this situation. Lastly, I believe they're not actually in Indonesia as they told you. I believe they flew to Port Moresby, where I'm quite sure George's father is still living. This being the case, at this stage, we are unable to extradite them given we have no extradition agreement with Papua New Guinea. Unfortunately, this means that our hands are really tied at the moment. I mean, they will only be on a tourist visa so they may have to move countries after a few months but, you know, with some of these places, money talks, and a lot of their immigration isn't really policed. Certain visas can be obtained for the right price, basically. There is a warrant out for their arrest and if they step foot in Australia they will be arrested and also, if they enter a country that we have an extradition order with, we will be contacted and they can be arrested and then extradited. But the situation is tricky – not hopeless, but tricky. I will do my best to find them and get the justice you deserve but we have to be realistic also.'

The detective's face changed to display a resigned look after his statement as Helena rubbed my back. I ran my hands through my hair, exhaling loudly. A hush over all of us followed.

'I just can't believe any of this,' I eventually whispered.

Helena wrapped her arms around my neck and kissed my cheek. I could tell that she was trying to suppress her visible sadness; however, I noticed the stifled tears that welled in her eyes, along with a subtly forlorn look. The detective waited a moment for all of this to unfold before he cleared his throat again.

'Well, I best be off,' he announced as he rose from his chair swiftly. 'There is much more to do for this case. Please, take care of yourselves. I will keep you updated on everything that occurs. And please don't hesitate to contact me if you need anything.'

We both looked up at him blankly and nodded from our seats.

'I'll show myself out,' he said as he left abruptly.

We listened to the door close behind him before I turned to Helena and hugged her. I could feel her cold ear on my cheek as she began to snivel, jolting softly from her quiet tears that were a combination of utter despair and fatigue.

The day then proceeded to pass in a blur of exhaustion, in a state where I was neither sure if I was awake or dreaming at times, the line between reality and fantasy becoming blurry to a clouded brain. A cloud of nervousness enveloped me as my body attempted to keep me awake with its sympathetic fight, flight or fright response. I attempted sleep throughout the day but the heavy drumming of an anxious heart made deliverance from this state by way of slumber impossible. Sleep did eventually find me that evening via a strong sleeping tablet that Helena had acquired from the chemist. It resulted in one of the most vivid dreams that I had ever experienced, quite the haunting nightmare in fact.

I dreamt that I confronted George in a nondescript location. A look of mortal fear painted his face as I wrapped my hands around his neck and squeezed hard, enveloped by a hot rage that coursed through me. I wanted him to experience the pain that I had; I wanted him to feel the sense of hopelessness that he had burdened me with. Harder and harder I clutched. I could feel the warmth of his neck on my hands as my grip tightened and I pressed with all of my might, trembling upon my exertion.

I watched with intense satisfaction as he struggled to breathe and fought for his life, his face growing more and more crimson with every moment. I watched the light leave his eyes as he took his last strained breath, failing to overcome my strength. He lay limply on the ground and I let out a defiant scream. I awoke, gasping in a cold sweat. Helena stirred but didn't wake as I sat up and mopped my brow, with the clarity of the dream still residing within me. I couldn't help but wonder if I was capable of that kind of rage, or of actions such as those that I had never thought myself capable of. I sat in the quiet bedroom for hours, wrestling with these thoughts in the partial darkness of the night-time. My tortured mind was such a prison.

Chapter 13
Thank You for the Venom

The day proceeding, I headed to the office in the morning. I felt the inclination to seek any signs that indicated the decline in my partner's conduct, conspicuous or not, that I may have overlooked in my blissful haze. I parked my car at the back of the office and sat there for a little while, in a cloud of exhaustion from the previous night's events that had made my sleep an erratic undertaking. My head was so foggy, my regular concentration and general thought processes evaded me. I studied my face in the rear vision mirror. My eyes appeared dreary, quite spiritless in fact, dark circles hung underneath to make them feel weighted.

The door opened with a creak to reveal the stilted silence of the building. Entering the office felt peculiarly enigmatic, like entering a crime scene or a derelict house that was once a place of serenity and joy, but now had a curious energy that clung to the air of it. It felt completely dissimilar: alien, almost.

I made my way into the space and moved towards my office. Standing in the doorway, I stared at my desk and contemplated all of the times when I would've been industriously labouring away, when all the while, my two comrades were plotting to stab me in the back. A feeling of woe sat side-by-side with a bitter resentment as I proceeded down the corridor, with the sound of my footwear on the floorboards seeming to echo more audibly than normal around the soulless edifice. I reached the desk and turned on the computer; that was when the phone rang, causing me to jump. Its startling resonation pierced the silence, every reverberation seemingly becoming more and more intense. I knew who it would most likely be: the man who had been repetitively ringing my mobile, Rocco Falcone. I deliberated on whether or not to receive his call, an act that I'd been dreading from the very moment that I'd seen his number first flash up on my mobile screen. Eventually, after a few seconds, I made the decision to answer, gulping as I picked it up.

'New Fullarton Builds,' I answered with the usual tagline.

'You finally decided to answer one of my fucking calls, did you?' Rocco's gravelly voice grunted.

'Rocco, I'm so sorry, mate. I've been flat out,' I stammered nervously, my heart rate increasing. 'A lot has happened these past couple of days.'

'I don't really give a stuff about your personal life, mate,' he responded abruptly, increasing his anger. 'All I care about is getting this reno done on my house. And the past two days, there has been no one bloody here! What the fuck is going on? I need to get this done!'

I paused and took a deep breath as my mind prepared its next statement.

'Okay, mate, I've got to be honest with you,' I spluttered in amazement that I was about to confront him with the news. 'So...'

I hesitated, contemplating how to breach the subject.

'This is bullshit, mate, tell me what the bloody hell is the hold up!' Rocco interrupted as he barked down the phone.

'Okay, so I found out a couple of days ago that George and his wife stole all the money from the company and have taken off overseas with it all. They're on the run.'

There was an audible grumble of displeasure, followed by a loud expletive from Rocco.

'You mean to tell me that you cunts have robbed me blind! I gave you a hundred grand cash upfront to get this shit done quickly and now you're telling me that I've got half a fucking house to live in and it's not gonna get done!'

'Rocco, I had no idea about any of this. I didn't even know that you'd paid George until the other day! I don't deal with the books. I genuinely didn't know anything!'

'Bullshit! You're both thieving bastards. You think I came down in the last shower, fuckwit?'

'Rocco, I promise I had no idea about any of this. I'm very sorry.'

'Yeah, you'll be sorry, alright,' he responded in a quietly eerie voice. He terminated our phone call gruffly.

I sat there for a moment and exhaled loudly with my heart pounding in my chest as I reminisced on our conversation. Unfortunately for me, I knew that it was not the last interaction that I would have with him, he was going to be the root of some major future issues. After trying my best to shake off the exchange, I decided that it was time to peruse the computer for any evidence of wrongdoing on Elaine and George's behalf.

I turned to the monitor and meticulously combed through every folder and document for hours but was unable to unearth a single morsel of evidence or clue. It seemed that they had disguised themselves thoroughly or at least been cunning enough not to leave any evidence in the office computer for me to uncover. I turned my attention to the pursuit of physical evidence and began trawling through the drawers of the desk, exhuming the junk and various printed files that they contained. Unfortunately, again, my search was fruitless. It was whilst conducting this search that a thunderous bang arose at the back door and I left the desk to stand at the foot of the hallway, discovering a perfectly horrifying sight. At the end of the passage stood a tall, stocky, immensely intimidating man in a hostile stance. He wore a balaclava with black jeans, a black leather vest atop a leather jacket and a red handkerchief around his neck, appearing to be a bikie member of some persuasion.

'Oi! Where the fuck is George?' he shouted angrily as he made his way down the hallway, brandishing a baseball bat that he held in his hand.

I backed away from the point that I was standing with both of my hands in the air, indicating that I would provide full cooperation under no resistance. He stamped his way aggressively down the passage to arrive at where I stood. I was greeted with a firm thud to the chest with an open palm, which forcefully moved me a few paces closer to the front window of the office. His eyes glared at me furiously, his clenched teeth the only other part of his face that I could visualise due to the abscondment from his balaclava.

'Where the fuck is he?' he screamed, aiming his finger fiercely at my face.

I stood for a moment in shock, trembling with fear and utterly petrified at the confronting sight. I attempted to verbalise a response; initially, words seemed unable to emanate from my mouth.

'I don't know,' I eventually muttered. 'I haven't seen him in a week.'

'Stop telling me fucking furphies!' he raged, his eyes widening as he yelled. 'You taking the piss out of me?'

'I'm not,' I replied, my arms still waving in the air in submission. 'I swear!'

He glared at me for a while, holding his fearful countenance before he backed away slowly, appearing to believe my statement. A cunning smile graced his face as he altered his grip on the baseball bat to clutch it with two hands.

'Okay, mate, well you give him this message.' He sneered. 'The cunt owes me fifty grand and has been ignoring me for a week!'

He proceeded to repeatedly swing the bat in the direction of the computer, annihilating it into pieces. He then tipped the desk over in a swift movement, causing it to crash onto the floor in a jarringly loud commotion.

'He has until Monday to pay me,' he advised in a quieter tone. 'And if I don't get it from him, I'll get it from you. I know you're his business partner.'

He exited down the hallway before I had the presence of mind to explain the logistical impossibility of his demand. Although, it was probably best to have kept discreet at the risk of infuriating him further or prolonging the situation. I would've struggled to get the words out anyway, given how arid my mouth had become. I heard the door slam and then the obnoxious sound of a motorbike engaging, which eventually faded into the distance. I stood there frozen with my hands still passively raised in the air. I was in disbelief at what had just happened, turning to survey the damage that was strewn all over the floor.

I fell to my knees and began to weep, the situation proving too overwhelming to a humble man. So many thoughts rattled through my tumultuous mind as I began to despair; my perfectly simple life had collapsed all around me and was fast becoming a gravely dire state of chaos. I had no money; my business was ruined and I was seemingly on the run from malevolent bikies. An immediate compulsion to escape flooded me to leave town and never come back. But this was quickly quashed with a sense of dismay; the criminal network probably had tentacles that reached far and wide, providing them with abilities to find those who didn't want to be found. A thought of the girls flashed in my head, jolting me to my feet. I had to get to Helena and Matilda to make certain that they were unscathed. I briskly left the building, arriving at my car, half-expectant to discover a shattered windscreen or somewhat impaired vehicle. Luckily, I found it intact. As I began the frantic journey home, I had the urge to contact Dennis and divulge to him what had happened, knowing that his advice in this situation would be paramount, given his years of police work and dealing with hardened crooks. He was ignorant of the entire situation as I had been compelled to keep everything a secret. Partly because of the humiliation and the fact that I was still striving to apprehend it for myself, but also because I was trying to keep my emotions in check. After a few rings, he greeted the phone in a cheery tone.

'Well, well, well! Thanks for calling me back, mate, I'm happy you're still alive at least!'

'I'm so sorry, mate, there's just been a lot going on.'

'Oh, right. Everything okay?'

'Nah... Nah, it's not. George has taken me to the cleaners. He's stolen all the money from the business and done a runner. I just had a bikie come to the office and smash up the joint because he owed them fifty grand. I'm a mess, mate.'

There was an audible gasp on the other end.

'You're kidding.'

'Wish I was.'

'Shit! Where are you?'

'I'm on my way home to make sure the girls are safe.'

'Okay, I'll meet you there.'

Chapter 14
Doors Unlocked and Open

Feverishly, I made my way into the house, travelling down the hallway and into the lounge room to where I heard some semblance of noise. Thankfully, there they were, safe and sound. Matilda was on the floor, happily playing away, while Helena was on the couch with a cup of tea in hand, watching her with the same exhausted look that we both shared.

'Are you both okay?' I cried, respirating heavily.

'Yes, yes we're fine,' Helena replied as she promptly put down her tea on the side table and got up to comfort me, appearing quite taken aback by my breathless state. However, before she got to me, my eyes caught the unlocked back door in horror and I frantically ran to lock it.

'Jack, what's wrong?' Helena inquired exasperatingly, rushing to me and grabbing my arms.

'Bikies,' I blurted.

'Okay, please just take a deep breath and calm down,' she soothed, leading me to a seat in the kitchen. 'Take a seat and tell me what's wrong.'

I complied and sat on the chair, taking in some deep breaths as she sat in the chair next to me. She gazed at my alarmed face, trying to take in the situation and provide the calmest response with her actions.

'A bikie came to work today and smashed up the place because they were looking for George. Apparently, he owes them fifty grand,' I informed, deliberately evading mention of the fact that I could possibly be made accountable for the debt. She gasped in response to my statement.

'My god, are you okay?'

'I'm alright. He didn't touch me at all.'

'Bloody hell,' she whispered as she began to falter, moving her hand to her mouth with tears welling in her eyes. 'What are we going to do?'

I wrapped her in a hug and held her consolingly. She sobbed quietly for a few moments before we eventually reconvened our conversation.

'I called Dennis and told him. He's on his way,' I returned as we untangled.

'You need to call the detective,' she said with a sniffle.

I turned and picked up his card that still sat on the kitchen table to study it; her suggestion hadn't actually crossed my mind previously in my state of panic. I kissed her on the forehead and stood up from the chair to retrieve my mobile phone from my pocket, during which, I realised that I hadn't greeted Matilda. I immediately remedied this by scooping her up and squeezing her tightly, with an audibly exultant groan on my behalf. I furnished her little face with kisses before placing her back in the spot that she had occupied previously.

I made my way up the hallway as I dialled the detective, removing my keys from my pocket with my free hand and double-locking the front door. After informing him of the events that had occurred, he apprised me that he would be at our house as soon as he could possibly be. I set about the two front rooms either side of the corridor, ensuring that the widows were fastened securely and the blinds were drawn to obscure an outsider's view. I moved to our bedroom to do the same, and once I was satisfied with my frantic endeavours, I made my way back to Helena to inform her that the detective would be over before long. Dennis arrived shortly after this, his face appeared subtly concerned as he greeted me when I unlocked and opened the door.

'Mate, I'm so sorry,' he said sympathetically as he embraced me.

He wrapped Helena in a hug as he reached her as well before we all sat down at the kitchen table in a quietly sombre mood.

'I'm in shock,' he said after a small pause. 'How are you two holding up?'

'It's been rough,' I replied, moving my hand onto Helena's thigh and stroking it comfortingly. 'For both of us.'

'Are you in the mood to talk about it?' Dennis enquired tentatively. 'I understand if you don't want to.'

'No, mate, it's fine,' I replied gloomily, quite weary of drudging over the details but also feeling that he had a right to know. 'It all started when a cheque we used to pay Teddy bounced. I found out that there was no money in our business account because George and Elaine had stolen it all to pay for their gambling and drug habits and then had done a runner overseas.'

Dennis leant back in his chair, his eyes widening as he muttered an expletive.

'They also sold drugs and owe other people money,' Helena added sadly. 'The bank took their house.'

Dennis shook his head in disgust.

'That's why the bikie came today,' I continued. 'He wanted the cash that they both owe him.'

'Christ, I can't believe it!' Dennis said in a shocked tone. 'You've contacted the police, haven't you?'

'Yeah, we have a detective coming over soon,' I replied.

He sat wordlessly for a moment, eyes glazed over with a

hundred questions, but not wanting to probe too freely and irritate his shaken and clearly exhausted hosts.

'Okay, well, I'm not going anywhere,' he stated as he stood from his chair. 'I'm going to organise some dinner and Claire and I will spend the night here. I want to be here when the detective arrives and do whatever I can.'

Helena and I looked up at him appreciatively, quite happy to have some bolstered support in our troubled time. He walked around the back of us and gently placed his hands on our shoulders before leaving the room to make a call. When he returned shortly after, we had relocated to the lounge. He sat himself on the one-man chair next to the couch, appearing agitated at the recent revelations.

'Jacko, what about today?' he eventually asked. 'With the bikie.'

'Well, I heard a bang at the back door of the office,' I started, turning to him but keeping my arm around Helena. 'Then I saw this massive bloke standing in the hallway with a balaclava and a baseball bat. He came down the hallway and asked me where George was, told me that George owed him fifty grand and when I told him that I knew nothing, he smashed up the computer and pushed the desk over, then took off.'

'Unbelievable.' Dennis sighed. 'You poor bugger, you alright?'

'I'm okay, just really shaken, I can't go back there, mate,' I responded wearily, 'luckily, he didn't touch me, he would've punched holes in me if he did though, he was huge.'

Helena's clutch became fearfully tight and she nestled further into me. I squeezed her back and kissed the top of her head in consolation. Dennis' inquisition ceased; the television entertained itself with us all sat in front of it, not knowing what to say. Before long, the quiet was interrupted by a knock at the front door from the detective, who greeted me with his firmly comforting disposition after I unbolted it. He followed me down the hallway and into the lounge, where he greeted Helena and I introduced him to Dennis.

'Senior Constable Dennis Bishop,' he said as he shook the detective's hand.

'Nice to meet you,' he replied. 'Detective Nicholas West.'

'Shall we all sit?' I announced, gesturing to the kitchen table.

'You don't mind if I'm here, do you, Jacko?' asked Dennis, moving towards me.

'Of course not, mate,' I responded, giving him an affectionate slap on the arm.

We relocated to the table, where Dennis sat next to the detective, with Helena and I sitting opposite.

'Okay, so I understand there was an incident today?' Detective West began.

'Yes,' I answered as I cleared my throat. 'I was at the office today and a bikie broke in through the back door, asking for George. When I told him that he wasn't there and I didn't know anything, he smashed up the place.'

'Tell me exactly what he said to you,' the detective probed.

'He asked for George. I told him that he wasn't there and that I hadn't seen him in a week. Eventually, he appeared to believe me and then said to give him the message that he wanted his fifty grand, which is when he started smashing everything,' I recalled before hesitating as I was about to add one more bit of information.

'Something else?' the detective asked as he perceived there was more knowledge to communicate.

'He also said'—I paused, taking a big gulp—'that if he didn't get the fifty grand by Monday, that he would get it from me, one way or another, because he knew I was George's business partner.'

Helena shrieked as she became visibly distressed.

'Oh, Jack, they're gonna come after you?' she cried as she nuzzled into my chest.

I put my arm around her comfortingly, with the two law enforcers staying relatively stoic; although, Dennis shifted in his chair, his eyes widening minutely.

'Mrs Newton, please calm down,' the detective advised. 'Let's not lose our heads here. Bikies, in my dealings, are unorganised and usually use scare tactics with empty threats. Would you agree, Senior Constable?'

'Yes, I would to an extent,' remarked Dennis, 'but a threat is a threat.'

'Yes, that is true,' the detective calmly harmonised. 'I think we better relocate you all for a little while, just as a precaution. Do you have anywhere you could stay for an extended period?'

'I think that's a good idea,' concurred Dennis.

'My parents,' Helena stated, moving from my chest to sit more upright to look at the detective, wiping her eyes and speaking in a more composed manner. 'They're back from holidays tomorrow.'

'Okay, I think you should make arrangements with them,' the detective implored. 'I will investigate your office and see if I can find anything that might give us clues on who it was. Do you have CCTV?'

I shook my head.

'It's okay, someone near you might. I'll check it out,' he notified. 'Just focus on getting your stuff together and relocating for now.'

'My wife and I will be staying here tonight with them as well,' Dennis said.

The detective turned and nodded in his direction.

'Lastly, can you just give me a rough description of the man,' requested the detective. 'Was he wearing any logos that you could recognise associated with a particular gang?'

'I didn't notice any, to be honest,' I replied. 'I was really shaken up.'

'Did he hurt you?' the detective enquired.

I shook my head.

'Okay, try and describe him for me,' he probed further.

'Well, he was quite tall and bulky, really intimidating. He was all in black. Black jeans and boots and a leather jacket. I don't remember seeing any patches or logos on his jacket, or anything like that. He wore a black balaclava over his face. Honestly, that's it. It's all a blur,' I said, grimacing as I strained to remember every detail.

'No other discerning features?' the detective followed up.

'No, he was really well covered up,' I said as I shook my head defeatedly. 'His voice is the only way I would remember him. I'll never forget that voice.'

The detective scribbled away on his notepad for a little while as we all sat with bated breath.

'Okay, that's all for now,' he announced as he concluded writing and put his notes in his jacket pocket. 'Please, take care of yourselves.in the meantime. Jack, can I have the key to your office please?'

He gave a pleasant nod as he rose to his feet and proceeded to shake all of our hands in farewell, before I gave him the key to the office that I had removed from my keychain. I followed him to the front door and bolted it behind him as he departed. When I returned to the living room, I discovered Helena standing and staring out the back window of the kitchen in an animated discussion on the phone to her mother. Dennis stood from his chair and stepped towards me, putting his arm around me in a clasp laced with reassurance. I was truly grateful to have such wonderful support and felt a lump gather in my throat as he did this, indicating that I had the potential to burst into tears at any moment. I was really struggling with everything; my world was shaken at its core and I couldn't believe how quickly things had gone from normal to catastrophic.

'I'm here for you, mate, whatever you need, okay?' he soothed defiantly. 'No one is going to touch a hair on yours or the girl's heads, you hear me? Or they'll have me to answer to.'

I didn't respond but rather tapped his hand that rested on my shoulder, in a gesture of non-verbal appreciation. He released his hold on me and I picked Matilda up from the floor, who was happy as Larry with a dummy in her mouth. I rocked her in my arms as she looked at me with an adorable grin that I obligingly returned.

'Claire will be round after work,' Dennis informed. 'She'll bring us all some tea with her and we'll keep you company for tonight.'

'Great,' I responded gratefully. 'Thanks, mate.'

The day petered out slowly as the inside light of the living room faded to obscurity at the arrival of dusk. With the advent of artificial lighting came Claire, who appeared in the doorway with an overnight bag and containers of takeaway food.

'Jack, I'm so sorry,' she said with a sympathetic expression as she made her way over to me to gift me with a benevolent hug.

'Thanks, Claire,' I replied with a polite smile in an attempt to put on a brave face.

Helena then appeared next to me, having ended an emotionally informative phone call with her sister. She attempted to replicate a polite smile similar to mine; however, it was obvious that she'd been crying on the phone and her exhaustion was quite prominently written all over her face. She looked at Claire and her eyes began to well again; the poor creature was at the end of her emotional tether, having barely slept or eaten. Claire enveloped her in a hug and held her for a moment, rubbing her back and whispering her sympathies for the situation. This made my heart wretch.

'Babe, Claire has brought us all dinner,' I informed. 'We need to eat something.'

'Oh, you're a gem,' Helena snivelled as she ended their embrace and wiped her face.

We all sat down at the table to eat, with Dennis and Claire sorting all of the crockery and cutlery that was required. On seeing the food, I felt a pang of hunger and realised that I had barely eaten since the news had confronted me. We tucked into our meals quietly, with the clinking of forks on ceramic the most prominent feature of dinner time.

Helena and I weren't exactly good company that night, but despite our muteness, it was agreeably pleasant to have company in our hour of need. Dennis and Claire helped to improve the void in spirit that the household was suffering from; in all truth, they were a godsend.

After dinner, they cleaned up the dishes and helped with Matilda before abetting us with the packing of belongings in preparation for our forced relocation in the morning. As the evening wound later into the night, we wished each other a pleasant sleep, retiring to our respective rooms. Helena and I readied for bed before laying on our backs silently with our hands intertwined, pondering restlessly on all that had happened and all that could possibly be coming our way. She eventually took a sleeping tablet to help her to rest, while I resisted initially and watched her drift off. She looked so serenely beautiful while she slept; I studied her with such sorrow, wondering why this perfect human should have to experience such torment that she didn't deserve.

After tossing and turning in bed for a while and catastrophising about what could be responsible for every little noise that I heard, I eventually relented to taking a sleeping tablet as well.

I wasn't fond of them, due to the nightmare that I'd had during the previous evening's rest and the grogginess that they left with me upon waking. But tomorrow was a newfound day in which to deal with this Armageddon and I resigned to the fact that I was better equipped to fight with rest under my proverbial belt than none at all.

V.

The girl with the golden hair,

her hand slips from mine.

It seems my angel has her wings,

but here with me she cannot fly.

Chapter 15
I Will Possess Your Heart

I awoke in the morning with a familiar sense of medicinally induced grogginess and an anxiously beating heart that was readied in anticipation. I turned to my side to discover an empty space that would usually be occupied by the girl with the golden hair. She had left the bed undetected, presumably to comfort a waking Matilda. This was a phenomenon that seldom occurred, given that I was such a light sleeper and Helena would usually rouse me unintentionally when attempting to rise from our bed. I could hear the clanging of utensils upon pans and ceramics and the sound of subdued conversation coming from the kitchen, co-existing with the pleasurable gastronomic odour of bacon. I arose from bed, quickly dressed and made my way to the source of the clatter.

'Morning, mate!' Dennis said cheerfully as I discovered that his and Claire's cooking was the source of the commotion coming from the kitchen. 'We nicked up to the shops this morning and cooked up a ripper brekkie for you both. Including Claire's famous smashed avo!'

Helena was already seated at the kitchen table with Matilda next to her in her high chair, as I kissed them both hello and took a seat in a mild haze of drowsiness. I sat agitatedly, burdened by the fact that we both had to remain idle when all we wanted was to disappear to perceived safety. I gazed at Helena, who clearly held the same apprehensions. She looked so drained, with prominently darkened circles under her eyes. She returned a nervous guise while meekly eating a slice of toast. The cheery chefs brought over the last parts of their spread, one with bacon on a plate and the other with a bowl of smashed avocado and took a seat at the table with us.

'Dig in, guys,' Claire remarked cheerily. 'You need to eat!'

'Thank you for this,' I muttered, feigning a smile with a genuine expression of gratitude. 'Really appreciate it.'

'No worries, mate,' Dennis said. 'Although all your praise should go Claire's way. I did bugger all if I'm honest!'

I wasn't hungry but I commenced eating, continuing to exchange disconcerted looks across the table with Helena while Dennis and Claire attempted to liven the mood. Unfortunately for them, it was to no avail; our busy minds were not in the mood for forced conversation and were more focused on politely forcing down the food that they had gone to the trouble of making for us. After endeavouring for a while to eat amongst the nervous quietude, I sprang to my feet, no longer able to ignore the uneasiness of my desire for Helena and Matilda to leave the house in search of sanctuary.

'I really would feel better if Helena and Tilly were on their way,' I declared, trading a knowing look with Helena, who leapt to her feet and began to remove Matilda from her high chair. 'After that, I'll have something more to eat.'

Dennis and Claire looked a little surprised at this hasty movement but then Dennis returned an understanding look as he rose as well.

'Okay, Jacko, let's get them on their way,' he responded.

We all left the table promptly with Dennis advising me that he and Claire would secure the bags and that I should make my way to the car with the girls. I walked with Helena, who held Tilly in her arms, unbolted the front door and instinctively inspected for danger on the outside before allowing them both to disembark from the house. Helena put Matilda in her car seat as Dennis and Claire both emerged with their baggage and placed it in the boot. They both embraced Helena separately and bid her farewell before returning to the house to give us some time to ourselves.

The day was cool and an icy wind blew on us, cottony grey clouds spread across the sky to give a weakened illumination to the daylight. We embraced each other tightly in a firm hug that was laced with tenderness and stood for a moment in silence. I savoured her feeling of home; I drew in her scent and cherished the smell of sandalwood on a summer breeze.

'I love you,' I whispered in her ear.

'I love you too,' she breathed back.

We snapped from our momentary comfort in realisation that it was time that they best depart. Helena got in her car and drove off, displaying to me a brave face that attempted to cloak her worry. I observed the car fade away into the distance at the end of Harvist Street and turn away down the neighbouring road to begin the 30-minute journey to her parents' house. Their property in the hills was relatively close by and accessed by windy roads adjacent to steep hills, which provided amazing views when one was in the mood to appreciate them, and more importantly, safe refuge. My anxiety eased minorly after their departure. I felt that once the girls had reached their destination, they would be sheltered from peril. I then concluded that once I had eventually joined them in asylum, my mind would be further able to rest some more. But until then, uneasiness would be a constant companion.

I made my way back into the house and sat down at the table with Dennis and Claire, recommencing dining with more success and ferocity than my previous bid.

'How we feeling, Jacko?' asked Dennis, lifting his head while he continued to eat his breakfast.

'Better now that they've left,' I replied, biting down on a piece of toast.

'So, what's the plan of attack?' he quizzed.

I rubbed my weary eyes as I took a moment to think and employ my hazy brain into action.

'Well, let's finish eating, clean up, then bolt up the house and be off,' I outlined decisively.

'Sounds like a plan,' Dennis responded. 'How about when we're done, we clean up all of this and you have a shower and fix yourself up a bit?'

I looked at Dennis hesitantly.

'Trust me, you don't look too flash,' he said. 'You'll feel much better.'

I relented with an exhale and nodded as we continued eating with sparing conversation, the clanking of cutlery once again making up a large component of the noise, just as it had during last night's dinner. Eventually, after we had all had our fill, I departed the table to the bedroom as Dennis and Claire instigated a clean-up. On my travel through the ensuite to the shower, I caught a glimpse of myself in the mirror, which prompted me to do a double take. The mirror reflected a face that looked truly awful – haggard, in fact. I ran my fingers under my eyes in a quiet moment of astonishment. The darkened areas under them had a horrid gloom, with my usually hazel eyes reddened and bloodshot, lacking their normal sheen. My face looked greyed; unkempt facial hair besieged my cheeks and anterior neck. A nest of jet-black hair sat atop my weathered head, populated by sparse grey strands that had seemingly multiplied during the crisis. Defeatedly, I turned the shower on and hopped in after an adequate temperature was achieved; the water instantly felt refreshing on my skin as a slight sense of reinvigoration washed over me to reduce the distress that I was feeling. I tried my best to suppress the undesirable, swirling thoughts that rattled in my brain, focusing on a repeated mantra of reassurance. I continued to tell myself that once we were all together, we would be harboured from the threat of danger. But this was sadly an ostensibly unachievable task within a brain that couldn't help but dredge through all of the possibilities.

After showering quickly, I got dressed and made my way back into the kitchen, where Dennis and Claire were concluding their clean up.

'Much better, mate!' Dennis remarked as I entered, looking up from the sink.

'Feeling better?' Claire asked as she placed something in the cupboard.

'A little bit, yes,' I replied. 'Thank you so much for brekkie and cleaning up. I'm just all over the shop at the moment but I really appreciate all of this.'

'Of course!' Claire returned.

'Our pleasure,' Dennis added. 'You two would do the same for us.'

I began to make my way around the house, checking that the back door was locked and ensuring that all of the windows were fastened securely with blinds drawn. After doing this, I removed my bag from the bedroom and took it outside to my car, re-entering the house to Dennis proclaiming that the kitchen duties were completed. I announced an immediate departure, with my two allies promptly gathering their belongings from the spare room and quitting the house. I locked the front door and assembled with them out the front to say our farewells.

'Good luck with everything, Jack,' Claire said with a cuddle goodbye before turning to Dennis and advising him that she would meet him at home.

We both watched her as she promptly located her car and departed, waving farewell.

'Okay, mate, good luck with everything,' Dennis said as he hugged me. 'Make sure you let me know if you need anything, alright?'

'Of course,' I replied as our brief embrace ended. 'You've done heaps, mate.'

We walked to my car and I hopped in, both of us exchanging looks of apprehension before I pulled the car out and left.

Unfortunately, I was not journeying directly to the hills like I urgently wanted to. A torturous venture to the supermarket was necessitated on account of Helena's parents having been overseas for an extended period and us not wanting to inconvenience them with our presence. The drive felt agonisingly protracted as I grew increasingly impatient at not being with the girls. When I arrived, I found the shopping centre to be heavily colonised with the cars of Saturday shoppers and sparsely populated with vacant spots.

I methodically trawled through the rows, beginning closest to the building with the hope of being auspicious enough to claim a nearby park, before eventually relenting to park in the back stalls after a lack of fortune. I rushed into the supermarket to find it flourishing with activity; I desperately wanted to race around the aisles to rapidly acquire everything that I needed and leave, but I was burdened with an inability to engage a clear thought process due to my fatigue and worry. This led to what felt like an extended dawdle around the shop as I unceremoniously moved my way through the hordes of people that clogged the aisles, many of whom did not appear to be in any form of haste in the slightest. Although, admittedly it was most probably the mild panic that I was experiencing that made them feel so cumbersome.

In what felt like an immense amount of time, I eventually acquired substantial supplies and queued at the checkout. It meandered excruciatingly slowly before I finally reached the front of the line to pay for my groceries and hurriedly moved to load them in the car. As I hopped in, it suddenly dawned on me that I had forgotten to pack my laptop in my luggage, which was a begrudgingly necessary item to communicate with clients and access everything that my shattered work life contained. I had no idea how long we would be in the hills under an assumed cover of darkness for. So, after letting an expletive fly in frustration, I started the car and commenced the journey back home, more anxious than ever that my journey to the sanctuary had not begun.

I was nervously sweaty, leaning forward in my seat and unable to relax due to the additional barrier of my voyage. The lingering trip made an agonising crawl through suburban streets as the car began to swelter unseasonably. Upon arrival at home, I quickly disembarked from my vehicle and instinctively surveyed the street for signs of abnormality to indicate a threat before fumbling with my keys at the front door and gaining entrance. I habitually locked the door behind me and stood at the entranceway, taking in a deep breath to gain some composure and begin a mental examination for the location of my laptop. My murky memory began to whirl slowly, like an old desktop computer from the 90s, as it searched its depths for the answer. I began with the usual place of residence, unfortunately to no reward. A wave of urgency overwhelmed me and I began a frenzied sprint around the lounge room, messily moving furniture and displacing components of the house. I moved into the bedroom and began a frantic search in there, dislodging the majority of the contents of the room in my attempt. Again, my search was unfruitful. I ceased my harrowed activity and pondered for a moment, racking my weary brain once again in investigation.

I had definitely removed it from the office on the last visit and brought it back home, to that there was no doubt, but its next movements were unclear. That was when I thought of the small gap under our bed that Helena liked to put my laptop. I dropped to my knees and looked attentively under the bed; low and behold, there it was! I removed it from its hiding spot and placed the laptop on the bed before turning to survey the room in which I had remodelled in my panic. It was a proverbial Chinese laundry!

I felt a compulsion to quickly tidy it back to its original state, not wanting my family to return to a house that had been ransacked. This prompted me to hastily tidy the bedroom before moving to the rest of the house to conduct the same reparations. Eventually, after the house resembled a normal status, I reverted back to the bedroom to grab the laptop before my departure. There was suddenly a knock at the door.

I froze. A chill ran down my spine and my mind obtained its own conclusions as to who the culprit could be. I drew in my breath for a few seconds, holding it to prevent an exhale as I listened intently to any noise that could be perceived. After a few silent seconds, another knock was heard. It was much more strident than the previous one and was followed by a vociferous announcement that signalled the identity of those at the door.

'Police!'

My brow crumpled in bewilderment at this statement, speculating as to why the regular police were in attendance. I began to tip-toe along the hallway ever so slyly to the front door, not wanting them to be aware of my presence. I glanced through the peephole, half-expecting to see some semblance of ruffian on the veranda, yet there stood two police officers dressed in their distinctive blue uniforms. They waited patiently with firm looks attached to their faces. I stood motionless in thought, deliberating on if I should ignore them, or open the door and hinder my immediate travel plans. During this rumination, however, a third loud rap was made at the door, along with another authoritative announcement. This settled my decision to heed them as I opened the door and curiously greeted them both.

'Mr Jack Newton?' a male officer asked sternly.

'Yes,' I replied sheepishly.

'Mr Newton, are you married and have a child to a Helena Newton?' he continued.

'Yes, I do,' I returned, still perplexed as to their presence at my home and the tone of their inquiry.

'Ahem, Mr Newton, I'm not quite sure how to tell you this,' the officer began, 'but approximately one hour ago your wife and daughter were involved in a car accident in the hills on Beverly Drive, where their car left the road and made its way down the hillside.'

I gasped audibly. My head spun with a traffic jam of befuddled contemplation. I rummaged for words but struggled to formulate a response. My mind was in overdrive, flashing countless scenarios in its internal cinema.

'Are... are they okay?' I stammered weakly, the desiccation of my mouth making words difficult. 'Wh... where are they?'

The police officers both shifted nervously, displaying uncomfortable looks of hesitation.

'They died at the scene, Mr Newton,' a female officer eventually uttered.

The words hit me like a blow to my entire body, like a thunderbolt to my entire soul. My heart lurched so painfully that it felt as if it exploded in the process. I clutched it as I gasped for air, every cell in my body screaming for oxygen. My trembling legs buckled under the weight of the officer's catastrophic words and I crashed to the floor. I sobbed uncontrollably. I sobbed until my lungs burned. Intense nausea overwhelmed me. Dizziness enveloped me. I became shrouded in a complete absence of light. The darkness wrapped itself around me tighter and tighter, constricting me like a murderous snake and choking me until breathing felt almost impossible. The darkness irreparably defiled my world, its light and colour stolen forever, its soul destroyed beyond repair. Everything went black.

VI.

What's the point in going on,

when my heart feels like the setting sun?

It shimmered and shone for most of the day,

but watch it now as it slowly fades away.

Chapter 16
I Promise I'm Not Okay

After that moment, I was lost. Utterly lost. Alone. Broken. Hopeless. I felt completely devoid of any fragment of happiness in my life. I actually didn't think that I would ever experience joy again as I found myself residing in a dark hole that seemed never-ending. It felt bottomless. It felt as if I would never escape its clutches. A deep sorrowfulness clung to me. My heart hurt. It ached, as if it was literally broken, paining me as it pumped blood around my languid body. My body felt lifeless and I wondered if my heart was too broken to properly function. I wept and wept. Sometimes uncontrollably. I screamed a lot too. It would let all of the anger and pain out momentarily. At the very least, it made me feel as if my soul was still a part of me because those cries felt like they came from the depths of it.

A lump resided in my throat incessantly, which made me wonder if my pain had built a home and my throat was where it lived. It refused to leave me. Waking up was a grave and bitter disappointment; the realisation when I opened my eyes of another day on this pointless earth filled me with the deepest of melancholy. Not that I slept much; I would drift in and out of a drearily hazy consciousness. The unconscious and conscious meshed together into one tortured existence.

In the haze, I would see her. I would see them both. Only glimpses, as they didn't last long, but I would see them. It was like my brain was attempting some form of protection and would quickly withdraw their mental images if they appeared. If I saw them in my dreams, it would jolt me back into the real world with a painful thump. This is when I would scream. And sob with guttural cries from the depths of my soul. It caused a constant fear of sleep, as it was a seemingly elusive and burdening event. Elusive because I couldn't really have it and burdening because of what it brought with it. I didn't want sleep to come because I knew of the harrowing battle that would eventuate, so sometimes I would try and fight it. When I wasn't asleep, the mental restlessness made me crazy. I existed with unrelenting contemplations rattling around the expanses of my conscious thought. For days, I barely moved from my bed. I didn't talk. I didn't see the point; there was nothing left to say. I had nothing. There was no happiness in my life. There was no longer any light either. And nothing to communicate.

I lay in the darkness and wallowed in a pit of despair. I hated the reality of life. I hated the unfairness of it all. I despised the fact that good people like me could feel this depth of sadness, while the dregs of the earth could seemingly prosper after a life of sin. It filled my blackened heart with hate. And rage. And painful grief. I got to the point where I didn't want to live. I really wanted it to be over. But I was too physically weak to do anything about it.

Apparently, Dennis heard the news of the crash and sped around to my house when it happened. He found me on my bed, barely conscious, with the two coppers and some ambos standing over me. I don't remember that. Helena's parents and Lucy eventually came too. That I do remember. We didn't say much. We just wept together, hysterically. But after the tears were diminished, I achieved a sense of numbness to overt emotion and wanted to be left alone with my grief. Dennis was never too far the whole time. I didn't speak to him. I barely even looked at him but I knew that he was there.

Initially, he tried to talk to me, but quickly understood that

I had nothing that I wanted to say. There was nothing that we could say. So, then he relented to just placing a hand on me whenever he would enter my room to let me know that he was with me. It was his way of providing comfort at a distance. He would bring me food and water and force me to eat and drink. I would nibble and sip little bits but I was never hungry or thirsty. Morsels seemed to sustain me. I didn't need much. And I didn't actually care about life or death at that point in time. Actually, that wasn't true. I didn't care about life but I would've happily welcomed death. It made me think about my dad and everything that he had gone through. I easily understood how he'd ventured down the path that he had. I feared how close I was to the tipping point of becoming a voided man such as him. I could see myself going that way. I just wanted the pain to stop. I was an emotional ruin. I was truly not okay.

A few days after the incident, Dennis informed me about the details of the upcoming funeral. Those words rocked me; I genuinely didn't know if I could do it. I wasn't in denial about it, I just didn't know if I could say goodbye to the two people that I loved more than anything on the planet. I had to face the farewell of someone that I had committed to spending the rest of my life with and a miracle that had we created with that love. Frankly, I didn't know if I had the strength to say goodbye with the knowledge that my life would never be even remotely the same without them.

My world had lost its moon and all of its stars in the sky. It no longer had a sun to orbit; it had lost its warmth. It no longer had a shining light. It was dark and cold. It was loveless and devoid of energy. And the worst part of all, my heart no longer had a home.

Chapter 17
Different Names for the Same Thing

I tossed and turned in pursuit of sleep the night before the funeral, stuck in a stampede of thought that plagued my mind in the darkness of the bedroom. The thought of death hung over me as I wondered why its notion could provoke human beings to feel a certain sense of terror deep within, even though it was ubiquitous and inevitable in life.

Previously, I had hated the vague and ambiguous terms that people impulsively used when articulating death, but I could finally understand it. Using the word 'dead' when referring to the people that I loved was so final. It felt so permanent that it cut like a knife. Sugar coating it was a human's attempt to provide a comforting hope and be combatant to the fears of an unknown afterlife. For me, the gut-wrenching feelings that I was burdened with made me fearfully wish that the girls were at peace and indeed in a place like heaven. I hoped more than anything to see them again and that a compassionate, all-knowing being really did exist; one who would take care of them in a paradise until I arrived. It was a seemingly desperate plea from an agnostic mind as I lay in bed, with the minutes turning into hours and the night fading into daybreak.

I'd been awake for ages when there came a knock at my bedroom door and Dennis poked his head in the room. He was dressed in a suit and tie, with a distraughtly sombre look painted on his face.

'They'll be here in about an hour, Jacko, to pick you up and take you,' he informed in a dry tone as I regarded him for the first time in days. 'Do what you need to do to get ready and we'll make you something to eat.'

He closed the door and I gazed back at the ceiling, focusing on the ornate cornice in its centre where the light fixture hung from. I had studied every bloody square inch of that thing; I knew every bump and every curve of its intricacy. I felt like it knew every square inch of my pain. I had stared at it while I had suffered and it had stared back, intently gaping at the shell of the creature that lay under it. I began to sob quietly – not one part of me wanted to face the day; it was hard not to be daunted by its prospect. Most people would come and then go back to their normal lives but I couldn't. I was saying goodbye to my normal and bidding adieu to my life's purpose.

My breathing got heavier upon this realisation as my broken heart pounded in response, causing me to clutch my chest and writhe in the bed with a painful grief. I rode the discomfort, like a timid surfer on a malicious wave, before attempting to control my breaths and reduce the drumming of my heart. I wiped my tears away; inhale and big breath in, then exhale and big breath out. Despite the anxiousness of facing what this day held, I knew that I had to do it for them both; I was aware that if the tables were turned, Helena would have been strong enough to face it.

I rose from the bed and got to my feet, stumbling slightly due to the fact that weight-bearing activity hadn't been conducted frequently in the past few days. As I stood for a moment to regain my balance, I was graced by the familiar bitterness of being alive without them. I hated life. So much. The lump in my throat made itself known again. I began to well up but stopped myself with a deep breath of attempted reassurance that summoned all of the miniscule determination that I had residing within me. Drearily, I walked to my cupboard and opened it, rummaging through my various articles of clothing until I came to a suit and shirt.

I didn't want to wear a tie; it didn't matter to me one bit what I looked like. I had no interest in showering or even looking at myself in the mirror; my care factor for myself was null and void. As I began to put the ensemble on, a memory of the last time that I had worn it flashed in my mind. I took a heavy-hearted gulp and let the film play out in my head. I remembered being stood in roughly the same spot as I dressed for a wedding that we had both attended. Helena emerged from the ensuite, graced with the most pleasant perfume bouquet that emitted from a stunningly beautiful woman. She made her way behind me and kissed me on the neck, telling me how much of a spunk I was – her little superlative that she loved to use on me. It was a tenderly simple moment in a seemingly past life that was made up of moments such as that. I plunged back to reality, with my chest burning like it was being stabbed with a red-hot poker fresh from a fire, a feeling akin to being branded by my longing for Helena.

I had to pause and take a moment to fight the overwhelming feelings and thoughts that churned in the bedroom. I needed out of this room. I finished dressing and placed my hand on the doorknob. A deep breath, in and out, loud exhale. My wrist twisted slowly on the cold handle and I weakly made my way into the living area, where Dennis was sitting on the couch with Claire. They both looked up at me slightly aghast, clearly not knowing what to say before scrambling over to me.

'Good to see you, mate,' he whispered as he began to fix my jacket collar before patting my hair down.

He glanced down at my feet in the process and then peered back at my face.

'I'll grab your shoes and socks,' he added softly as he left for the bedroom.

Claire beheld me with a comforting guise, clasping me tightly without a word. I could barely squeeze back; I didn't have much strength left within me, given that I had barely stirred, let alone eaten in the past few days. The harrowing emotional battle had completely voided me of any vigour.

At that point, I began to feel shaky on my feet, which Claire could sense. She ended her hold on me and moved me to the couch, announcing that she would find me something to eat and drink. Dennis returned with shoes and socks and proceeded to put them on my feet, like a parent dressing their child prior to a big day at school. After he was done, he sat down beside me and patted my leg in a show of solidarity. Claire came over with a glass of water and placed it in my hands as they both then watched me intently to ensure that I didn't struggle. Upon observing a successful sip, Claire returned to the kitchen to continue the due diligence in her culinary efforts for me, while Dennis and I sat soundlessly on the couch.

The clock on the wall seemed to tick obnoxiously loud, audaciously reminding me of the imminent approach of the most agonising task that I had ever faced. The smell of toast became prominent, with the scraping of a knife over it transcending the depressing solace of the house. I nibbled on a piece of toast that was brought over and had a few more sips of water, which was all that I felt that I could manage without feeling sick.

Time passed slowly in the lounge room as we all sat and waited for the impending doom, with Dennis and Claire shifting nervously and only breaking their reticence to communicate with a whisper if it was required. Finally, there came a commotion outside, along with a knock at the door, which signalled the arrival of the other members of the funeral party.

'I'll get it, Jacko,' Dennis uttered quietly as he left the couch.

I didn't budge when the knock was heard. I think that my body was in the midst of attempting to tune down my senses in preparation for the funeral so as to make me emotionally numb to cope.

Initially, I stared blankly as they all entered the room, trying to compartmentalise everything that their arrival signified. However, my obliviousness was broken by the conspicuously grating sight that was unfolding in front of me.

Helena's father, Luke, braced her mother, Elizabeth, by holding her by the shoulders and guiding her. Lucy and Bryan followed behind them, shadowed by the stern-looking funeral director. Elizabeth was a very evident wreck. She looked dishevelled; her makeup had been ruined by the river of tears that flowed from her grimaced eyes. I stood to attention and beheld her struggle towards me. She was a woman in her early sixties, who shared the height and facial features of Helena; however, she was much rounder in figure and had light brown hair instead of the golden hair of her daughter.

She leant on her husband, a lanky, bald man who displayed solemnly glassy eyes, with a frown that sat below his rusty-coloured moustache. Lucy stood behind them; her face exhibited a pained expression with evidence of heavy tears. However, she appeared to hold her composure somewhat with a more controlled grief. Although, it was possibly the more riotous outward expression that her mother displayed that made her composure seem so much more heightened in comparison. They all wore mostly black, except her dad who wore a bright purple tie, which seemed to shine brightly in the noir-toned world that we currently existed in. I inferred that it was a tribute to Helena's favourite colour growing up, as her childhood room had been painted purple and decorated with an array of purple things.

Elizabeth collapsed into my arms, sobbing in my ear as I returned a lukewarm strengthened hug and strained to support her weight, slightly taken aback by her intense embrace. I really had no desire to share in an outpouring of grief. I still wanted to deal with it on my own, but on the other hand, I didn't want to be selfish to good people who were only dealing with things in a way that they felt was best.

'Oh, Jack!' she sobbed in my ear. 'I'm so sorry.'

She repeated these words a few times but they were muffled by her sobbing and I had switched off of discerning anything intelligible from her. After a few moments, I turned her and sat her down on the couch. I then limply clasped Lucy, feeling my eyes well as I held her but holding in my desire to cry. She began to weep softly as we hugged each other without speaking. There was no need for words or redundant questions. We both knew that we'd been in hell the past few days and didn't know where the exit was. I stiffly moved to her father after parting from Lucy for a firmer yet briefer embrace, which then was repeated with Bryan.

'We probably should get going, everybody,' the director announced softly I shifted over to Dennis and Claire, who stood away from everyone, observing cautiously.

'Is there a hearse out there?' I whispered waveringly, leaning into Dennis.

His face dropped as he looked at me grimly and nodded. My lip began to quiver. I grew shaky on my legs once more, which Dennis noticed and quickly grabbed my shoulders to hold me upright.

'I can't do it,' I mouthed silently. 'I can't see it.'

'I'm going to walk you to the car,' he whispered as looked at me reassuringly. 'Keep your head down, I got ya.'

He then placed his arm around me to support my weight and drew me close to him, just as he had done many times, as we began to make our way slowly down the corridor. I closed my eyes as we reached the door and listened to him open it. Our footsteps hit the timber veranda as an icy wind blew on my face with each step towards the car. We trod forward. I kept my eyes fastened, moving off the veranda, along the paving, past the footpath and onto the road. My head galloped with images of what was most likely unfolding in front of me. The thoughts made me falter slightly, my strength seemingly zapped trying to combat them all. But luckily, Dennis was right there with me every step of the way.

'Almost there, Jacko,' he murmured with his voice crackling slightly.

I heard the door of a car open and I was directed inside, moving along the leather seats of the back to the far side window, keeping my eyes to the floor. I rested my forehead on the front passenger-side seat, sitting motionless as a sniffling Lucy took her station next to me and placed her hand on my leg in comfort. I wanted to return the favour but I simply didn't have the strength. Helena's father then steered her mother into the front seat and took his spot in the back on the opposite side of Lucy. Elizabeth appeared to have ceased her loud sobbing for the meantime but audibly sniffled to break up the silence in the car. The funeral director took his place in the driver's seat and we began our journey.

I tried to block out the sounds of crying as I attempted to emotionally fortify myself, wanting to transport myself to a faraway place where I could deal with things on my own. But no man is an island. I clearly needed the support of others and was affected by the emotions of those around me. Plus, the impending conclusion of our current passage loomed and made detachment obstinate. I simply couldn't numb myself. Tears fell from my cheeks as we crept along, with the others whimpering in a morose hush. Not one word was uttered for the drive to the cemetery. I hated that moment more than anything in the world. I hated it a million times more than the journey after finding out that I was bankrupt or the journey after being threatened with my life by the bikie. Those were a picnic on a tropical island compared to this dire shipwreck.

Chapter 18
Ingenue

The journey to the cemetery chapel was probably a short journey in terms of kilometres or minutes, but to me, it felt like a tortuously long ride. One of mental and physical anguish where my eyes were obscured by the watery blur of tears and the sound of silence was prevented by weeping. While my mind's tranquillity was absconded by a movie of my life that was playing in its cinema. The star actress had lit up the screen with her angelic smile and sparkling green eyes that had made her seem like surreal perfection. Eventually, the car pulled up out the front of a small, light-bricked building that was nestled amongst the trees and gravestones. We all hesitated before getting out. The others disembarked before me; Luke left his seat first and made his way to the front of the car to help Elizabeth out, while Lucy left after them. I watched the three of them make their way into the chapel amongst a crowd of sympathetic onlookers. I paused and took some deep breaths in preparation for the emotional summit before leaving the vehicular sanctuary to stand weakly on my feet.

I felt the burn of eyes on me but refused to meet the gaze of any person that they belonged to. My concentration was intensely focused on achieving the emotional numbness that I had been willing to accomplish previously. I felt that if I was able to float through the funeral with a lack of presence, then it would conclude relatively quickly and I could get back to grieving alone without the company or pity of others. After a few moments of solitude, I felt that I had achieved a relative impassiveness. I could barely feel the temperature on my skin, while my face was empty, with a mouth devoid of expression and eyes that felt inanely lifeless. My mind was my only downfall. It would flash frequent reminders of the present situation, along with various arbitrary memories, in a seeming attempt to remind me of what was occurring and substantiate a worthy emotional response. While this internal war raged, I floated into the chapel and up the aisle, staring vacuously in front of me as I moved. I focused on steps, on breathing, on detachment, as I took my seat next to the family on a rigid pew. The priest began to talk. I moped, knowing how much Helena would've hated the religiousness of it all. Unfortunately, I hadn't been in the state of mind to contribute to any of the planning.

Vacantly, I stared out into the distance, in a seemingly unemotional nirvana. I was numbed sufficiently to the reality of the situation for the time being, with the muffled sound of God's helper playing softly in the background.

But then came time for the eulogy and Lucy got up to speak. Suddenly, I became more aware of the hardness of the wooden pew. Nirvana slipped away. My ears were able to pick up her voice clearly, my mind evidently feeling that this was the part of the tribute that I needed to pay attention to. The congregation and I began to hear about how Helena, nee Somerset, was born in one of Melbourne's leafy eastern suburbs to an honest, middle-class family. We heard that she was a beautiful child who had grown to become a truly amazing woman; she was quiet and calm, kind-hearted and generous, loving and endearing. We were told that she had contemplated a career as a nurse because she had wanted to help people but had settled on studying physiotherapy at university. She had excelled in her studies and eventually gained a job that she adored, with patients that simply cherished her. Then my name was mentioned and the congregation was informed of a small snippet of our story.

Lucy outlined how Helena had met a man by the name of Jack Newton at a bar, who had luckily had enough drunken courage to give her his number in a public way; how she had confessed to her sister that she may have found 'the one' and soon after confirmed that this was the man that she wanted to marry and have kids with. Finally, Lucy told how Helena had emphatically said that marrying me and having Matilda were the two greatest achievements of her life.

That's when I became aware of the lump again; the home of sorrow. Swallowing was heavy and painful, gulping for air was an arduous task. My lip quivered. My eyes welled. The dam wall was breached and I couldn't prevent it from breaking any longer. I began to bawl.

I tried to be quiet but I had to gasp for air and once it was let out, it wouldn't stop. My sorrow was dished out for all to see; all of the feelings that I had tried to ignore surged out of me completely involuntarily. My heart burned. I clutched it because it was so sore. I moved my palm to my mouth to stifle my cries as a river of tears continued to flow, drifting against my hand before they trickled onto the carpet. I leant forward to stare at the floor in an attempt to gain some equanimity and remedy the nausea that I was beginning to feel.

Lucy concluded her eulogy and returned to sit back down next to me, putting her arm around me and sharing in my tears. Again, I couldn't respond or reciprocate with any form of gesture. I was barely there. The movie had commenced again and played out in my head. I was meeting her at the bar; I was on our first date; I was kissing her for the first time; I was proposing; I was at our wedding; I was in the hospital holding Tilly; I was hearing Tilly speak for the first time; I was walking in from work and seeing them together. It was all there right in front of me.

I don't recall the rest of the service. I just remember being informed that it was over and floating down the aisle whilst once again looking down at the path in front of me and avoiding eye contact with anyone. The burst of cold air was a relief upon exiting the stifling atmosphere of the chapel. I travelled quickly to the same car that we had arrived in and entered to sit in silence with a loud exhale. I was well aware that people would have wanted to offer me their condolences but I didn't want them. I just couldn't face the task of dealing with people who pitied me or having to feign gratitude through the bravado of a brave face. Eventually, the rest of the sombre party joined me in the car and rescued me from the anguished world that I had been trapped in while waiting. I met Lucy's forlorn gaze as she entered and sat next to me, clutching my hand to squeeze it.

'Good job on that eulogy, Luce,' I murmured.

'Thanks, Jack,' she whispered back.

We all sat in silence on our journey to the wake. Our glassily dreary eyes stared out into the distance through the window, viewing the world that was happening around our grief-stricken one, but not really computing anything that was being observed.

The wake was at my local football club, who had organised it as a tribute to our family. We had spent so much time there that we were almost part of the fabric.

As we arrived, I miserably beheld the large brick building, painted in a cream colour, with the dark, sun-kissed, tin roof and terrace that ran around its perimeter. This place usually represented joy; happiness had once made up the foundations and been ingrained into the structure. But on this day, it had all seemingly disappeared. I left the car with the family and we made our way into the club as people were starting to arrive in the car park, while a few had already gathered in the rooms.

The small foyer of the building opened into a bigger social club space, which was filled with large tables and chairs, while the walls were adorned with pictures of premiership teams, premiership flags and sponsor advertisements. It had served as such a fortress of happiness and joy in my life; I was one of those smiling men in the pictures on the wall. But this time, it was a dark hole, a lifeless void of a place. The room was inert and lacked any form of vibrance that it usually contained for me. The air was stale; it felt like a place where enjoyment could never possibly exist.

I made my way to the bar and was given a beer by the club president. I glanced at him with a telepathic 'thank you' and a nod of the head, while he expressed his sympathy wordlessly with a warm slap on the shoulder. A couch on the far wall from the bar became my haunt. I sat with my eyes glaring unemotionally towards the floor so as to not make eye contact with anyone and hopefully render myself unapproachable. Eventually, my daze was broken by Dennis and Claire, who took a seat either side of me. Dennis put his arm around me and Claire leant on my shoulder, in an act of unwavering succour from both of them.

'Got you, mate,' he uttered.

Shortly after, Ted, Pilks, Bewsy, Chewie and Royce appeared before me with beer stubbies in their hands, all with their partners in tow, to render their subtle condolences. They were armed with sombre looks on their faces and all took turns to make me aware that they were present with me in bolstered solidarity. I acknowledged their support through gloomily crimson eyes.

'Jacko,' Pilks said hesitantly as he broke the muteness, 'me and the boys have been talking and if you're okay with having us, we wanna stay at yours tonight with you.'

'Just to help in any way we can,' Bewsy continued soothingly while the others nodded in agreeance.

'We'll get through this together, one day at a time,' Dennis added as he gripped me tighter.

'No need to go through it all alone, Jacko,' Chewie adjoined in a crackly voice.

'You'd do the same for us, mate,' Royce attached.

Once again, the sorrowfully protuberant section of my throat sprang to action. My lip trembled with the quiet tears that started to flow. It was an emotional outpour of gratitude for their overwhelming support and adulation at the fact that I had such amazing people still present in my life.

'Thanks, boys,' was all I could mutter.

However, they understood my utterance to be an affirmative to their request and resumed their dismally reserved interactions with one another. Those two words were the most prominent ones that I spoke during the entire time at the wake. The day played out like a movie scene in which the protagonist stayed dormant for the entire act, while more vigorous activity took place all around them.

I sat and stared emptily, occasionally moving the beer that I nursed in my hand to my lips, while people quietly and politely chatted around me. I muttered thankyous and feigned the occasional half-smile at mourners who came over to pay their respects. I weakly squeezed outstretched hands and stood to give lukewarm hugs. But I completely avoided engaging with anyone as I normally would. The boys and their partners stayed in my presence the entire time and formed what felt like a protective cocoon of obscurity around me for the duration of the wake.

The day passed in a relative blur, with Dennis and Claire driving me home on its conclusion. I was exhaustedly drunk. My groggy eyes could barely open and my mind was emotionally drained. I collapsed on my bed after being ushered into my house by the members of my support network. My heart ached terribly. It had been working overtime all day with its intense beating. While my body felt shattered from attempting to move and function as a being who was not indeed as lifeless and soulless as he felt.

As I drifted off to the sound of a low ruckus in the living room, I was aware that the hardest day of my life was officially concluded, which was a mild relief. However, the inauguration of the rest of my persecuted existence on this earth alone was a daunting prospect to even a drunken mind.

VII.

I'm all out at sea,

my mind won't be.

She's a breach of my wake,

she's a breach of my dream.

A lover,

like no other.

She's a breach of my soul.

She's a breach I'll never cover.

Chapter 19
I Dreamt We Spoke Again

In my dreams that night I saw them. I saw them both so vividly. They looked so beautiful and utterly perfect. In the dream, I awoke in my bedroom to hear pleasant sounds coming from the lounge room; one was the intonation of a gentle woman and the other was the cooing of a sweet child. They sounded so happy and peaceful. The bedroom was shrouded in its usual darkness, with the only form of brightness permitted through the gaps in the doorway and the sides of the curtains. I sprung to my feet and rushed to the door to open it. And there they were, my two flawless creatures. Upon entering the lounge and seeing them both, I discovered the light in there to be so brightly vibrant. It shone lustrously on them both. It was as if the world had gained its luminosity back and was a place worth living. A place where living things could thrive once again because the sun had returned from its dormancy. A world where I could blossom once again because I had my light back and I could see it in all its wonder. The bedroom had felt cold, but the lounge felt so warm and loving with this luminescence. I felt an overwhelming happiness and an exaltation of joy. My heart felt warmly fuzzy; I vibrated a little with the fuzziness, cherishing the cosy sensation on my skin. Helena held Matilda in her arms, as they stood in a gentle glow, both dressed in white. I rushed to them both and embraced them tightly. Tears of happiness flowed down my cheeks. I could feel the warmth and tenderness of their touch and the softness of their skin on mine. I kissed Matilda's sweetly soft cheek and then Helena's supple lips; they were just as I had remembered. Helena and I rested our foreheads on one another with our noses touching and stared deep into each other's eyes. Her porcelain skin was faultless and felt so delicate on mine, her eyes were the most beautifully precious emeralds that a man had ever laid his own eyes on. We gazed into each other, glaring into each other's souls, without one word being said. The moment was perfect. The complete and utter joy. The warmth and tenderness. The glow of my two angels. The light that had returned to the world. The vibrancy. The fuzziness. Everything was as it should be. The world was right.

'Everything is not as it seems,' Helena whispered in her angelically safe tone, as she broke the silence ever so slightly.

I didn't give her sentence much umbrage, as I was ensconced in the feeling that endowed me and simply enamoured by the sound of her voice. She grabbed my hand and led me down the hallway to the front door. Her hand wrapped in mine; it fit so impeccably, like it was made to be there. It was so soft and delicate, yet so secure. She led me outside to her car; the sky was the most unblemished powdery blue, adorned with a vibrant orange-red coloured sun. It felt as warmly nourishing as it had felt inside, the world was so silently peaceful. It was so contented and pure. I got in the car, while Helena placed Tilly in her car seat in the back and then got in the driver's side. As we drove, I looked back at Tilly. She was so blissful and had the most gorgeous smile on her face. I gave her my index finger and she clutched it tightly, as she stared at me. She had the most adorable green eyes and golden hair; my heart was full of endless love, exultant at the fact that Helena and I had created something so truly delightful. The glow from the outside light that fell on her made her look like an angel; just as her mother had appeared to me so many times. Suddenly, before I knew it, the car had stopped and I turned to see that we had arrived at the funeral chapel. It looked so different compared to the day of the service; it was alluring and basked in the exquisite glow of the light from the sky. Its light-coloured bricks were a glistening gold. Helena grabbed Matilda from the back of the car and then made her way to me, clutching my hand as she led me from the car into the chapel. It was empty, but it glowed inside; every part of it shone in the most amazing golden hue. We walked down the aisle, with Helena's wondrous touch guiding me every step of the way. She looked back at me with an adoring smile. She was so truly divine and shone in the gilded glow of the chapel. We stopped when we got to the end of the aisle and stood just before the altar. Helena turned to me and kissed me lovingly, her soft lips felt like silk on mine. Again, we gazed silently into each other for a moment, before Matilda interrupted with a kiss on my cheek. I embraced them both and basked in their heartfelt presence, squeezing them both tightly.

'Everything is not as it seems,' Helena whispered again in my ear during this embrace, as I closed my eyes in an attempt to savour the true ecstasy of the moment. The instant that I did this, I felt them disappear into thin air. I could no longer feel their touch. I opened my eyes suddenly to see nothing in front of me. I stood aghast; the chapel was now dark and sombre. Outside, a dim moonlight provided a weak glow that placed the inside of the chapel in a mysteriously eerie shadow. There was no golden radiance; it was a truly bleak place full of death and emotional torture. It was an evil, wicked place that robbed people of their loved ones. It felt icily cold, my breath was visible as I exhaled. I rushed down the aisle in distress, bursting through the chapel entrance doors to the outside. The night was chilling and dark. The sky was almost pitch black, with a muted, small moon that provided a minute amount of light. I no longer felt warm and fuzzy or vibrant and content. I felt complete and utter despair and pain. This world was now dull and joyless. I collapsed to my knees and let out a guttural cry; a blood-curdling scream of rage induced and sadness.

Chapter 20
A Lack of Colour

Suddenly, I awoke into the real world in a cold sweat. My heart thundered against my ribcage. I was abruptly thumped with a familiar feeling; intense sadness, not wanting to be alive, the dread of waking up, the unbelievably heavy heart, the lumped throat – it was all still within me. I pounded my fist on the mattress in jaded disbelief at having Helena and Matilda ripped away from me once again. I began to cry, a crucifying mixture of anger and sorrow swelled violently within me.

I lay there for a while and let the raw tears flow before leaving the bed to drag my heavy heart and body to the shower. After ensuring that I didn't catch a glimpse of myself in the mirror on the way through, having no immediate desire to see the shell of a person that I'd become, I turned the shower on and waited miserably for the water to heat up. The water felt pleasant, like it was cleansing my body of some of the cells that contained the displeasure that had cleaved me. It provided me with a sense of comfortable warmth that I had not felt in a while.

The shower steamed the room, fogging the glass screen and mirror. It took me back to days when Helena and I would make love in the shower, almost to the point of passing out from the humidity. I had always marvelled at the suppleness of her skin on mine as we danced about the shower passionately; the silkiness of her hair would change to a ruddy blonde when wet, like melted gold. My heart burned at the longing for her touch;

nothing pleasant brushed my fingertips. All I could feel was the slipperiness of the tiles and the coarsely rough grout that was woven in between them.

Eventually, I turned the shower off and towelled down before deciding that I wanted to confront my reflection. I stepped in front of the mirror above the vanity. I wasn't shocked by what I saw; it revealed what I had expected. A gauntly soulless man stared back at me. He looked old and weathered, corpse-like. I barely recognised him. The reflection was left to linger for a moment before I proceeded to brush my teeth to rid them of their grittiness.

As I got dressed, I could hear the slight murmurs of the guests in my lounge room, along with the lulling babble of the television. I grabbed the doona and draped it over myself to leave the room, opening the bedroom door to discover my three new housemates. Bewsy and Pilks were seated on the couch, while Chewie was seated in the single-person chair next to that. They all turned and looked up with sympathetic faces, standing as I entered and greeting me with a delicate cheerfulness.

'Morning, Jacko,' Pilks greeted, reaching his hand to pat my back.

I continued to the middle of the couch and sat, with them all proceeding to take their seats again.

'How you feeling, old mate?' asked Bewsy.

'Same old,' I muttered in response.

'Now, Jacko,' Chewie said as he left his seat and went into the kitchen. 'I've been to the servo this morning and got you a Gatorade and a pie. I know how much you love them both the day after drinking.'

I softened at the gesture, which was somewhat touching. Chewie returned with a pie on a plate, adorned with tomato sauce, and set it on my lap along with an orange Gatorade that he placed at my feet. I looked at the pie. I hadn't had a meal this big in days. A twinge of hunger hit my stomach as it gurgled, seemingly screaming for nourishment.

'Thanks, Chew,' I murmured as I looked up at him earnestly.

'No worries, buddy,' he said. 'Get that in your gob and you'll feel like a million bucks.'

I began to nibble away slowly. They all watched me fixedly before quickly realising that they were all examining me too closely and promptly initiating a conversation to ease the awkwardness.

'Good work, Jacko,' Bewsy praised. 'Any good?'

I nodded as I gnawed away at the pie.

'You could've at least gone to the milk bar or bakery and got the man a decent pie, Chew,' Pilks teased in an attempt to lighten the mood.

'Oh, piss off, Pilks!' Chewie said. 'Me and Jacko aren't pretentious dead shits like you!'

The pair sitting either side of me laughed while I continued to eat, unable to muster a smile. The laughter subsided with a brief pause.

'So, the other two were here for a bit last night but they both had to work today so they didn't stay,' Pilks informed, referring to Dennis and Royce. 'They'll be here a bit later. The rest of us bludgers have taken the rest of the week off so you're stuck with us for as long as you want us here.'

I picked up the Gatorade bottle from the floor and undid the cap, taking a sip and feeling the cool orange liquid pleasantly slide down my arid throat.

'Great,' I replied meekly after a big gulp.

'The footy's on tonight. They said they'll be 'round for that,' Bewsy outlined. 'So we'll organise a bit of tucker for lunch later, then lounge around here and do whatever. I'm thinking fish and chips. A couple of dimmies and potato cakes would go down a treat.'

'But, Jacko, before that, I've got something for you to get the day started right,' Chewie announced with a mild exuberance as he proceeded to pick up the remote and change the setting from the normal digital television.

On the screen flashed a YouTube clip that read: 'Shane Warne's Top 10 Wickets'.

I'd once stated that watching any of S.K Warne's classic wickets could always lift me out of a funk, but unfortunately for Warnie, this would be a tough task. The intense sorrow that I was experiencing was one that not even the great man would be able to dismiss with any of his mesmerising deliveries.

Chewie cheered softly as he pressed play on the video in a noble yet arduous effort to lift my mood. Although I did greatly appreciate the gesture, an effort to even feign a smile was just too great. I did my best to look up at him with grateful eyes, which was the greatest form of thanks that I could provide to him. Thankfully, he appeared vindicated by it.

'Watching this reminds me of when I rolled the arm over to you in the nets at school, Bewsy, and sent your stumps cartwheeling,' Chewie said after viewing a few wickets.

'Get stuffed!' Bewsy retorted. 'You're such a bullshit artist, there's so much mayo on that story. It happened one time when I was taking the piss while I was facing you. I think I even had my eyes closed because of how shithouse you were.'

'Or were you scared and closed 'em because you're weak as piss and knew I bowled express pace?' Chewie questioned facetiously as Pilks chuckled.

'You're ruining Warnie's wickets with all your porkies,' Bewsy remarked.

'Jacko knows the truth,' Chewie said as he ruffled my hair lightly. 'No one gives a fat rat's clacker about your excuses, Bewsy!'

I nodded politely in response as I cast my mind back to the day when were fifteen or sixteen years old and had gone to the nets to try out for the high school cricket team. Chewie, who had not been blessed with great cricketing prowess, had bowled to Bewsy, the opening batsman for the school team at the time. The ball that he had bowled had been so slow that it had almost bounced twice. Bewsy had tried to cut it squarely, but in the process, had chopped it onto his stumps. The nets had erupted in laughter, with Chewie celebrating exuberantly as Bewsy hung his head in a jovial shame. From that point on, it had gone down in the annals of our friendship and was re-hatched whenever its relevance was deemed necessary.

'Let him have it, Bewsy.' Pilks laughed. 'You know he'll never let go of it, no matter how hard you plead your case.'

'Good call, John,' Bewsy replied. 'Gotta let the nuffy have something over me.'

'I got plenty over you,' Chewie claimed.

'Like what?' Bewsy enquired.

'I'd rather not embarrass you in front of the boys.' Chewie grinned impishly.

There was a loud tap at the door. We froze for an instant, glancing at each other and not knowing what to do.

'Want me to get it?' Pilks whispered, being closest to the hallway.

I nodded in affirmation as he got up and walked to the front door. Upon opening it, we heard a happy acknowledgment from Pilks to the perpetrator and craned our necks to see Ted standing in the open doorway. The two marched in and Ted greeted us all, holding a large tray in his hands that was shielded with aluminium foil. He proceeded to take it over to the kitchen and place it on the bench.

'Jacko, the misso made a big fuck-off tray of lasagne for you,' he advised as he opened the fridge and made room for it before placing it in.

'Oh, great. Thanks, mate,' I mumbled.

'She makes a grouse lasagne, too, so you're in for a bloody treat, I reckon,' Ted said as he moved to the lounge, commandeering a chair on his way and noisily relocating it.

He sat and paused for a brief instant, wanting to avoid asking the superfluously rudimentary question of 'how are you?'

'What we up to, boys?' he asked.

'Bugger all, Teddy,' Bewsy responded. 'Just watched Shane Warne vids on YouTube.'

'Classic.' Ted laughed. 'You blokes are all bludging from work the rest of the week, aren't you?'

'Sure are,' Pilks answered. 'You got no work on either?'

'Well, I just quoted a job near here, then thought I'd quickly duck home and drop this lasagne off to Jacko. But yeah, I'm free for the rest of the day. Since George played funny buggers and took us for a ride, I've got a bit of a gap in work 'til the next job.'

'Sorry to hear about all that,' Pilks sympathised.

'Oh well, can't cry over spilt milk, no matter how bloody filthy I am about it, you know?' Ted sighed. 'Stitched us both up, didn't he, Jacko? Pulled the wool right over my eyes, that's for sure.'

'My oath,' I said.

'He's an absolute mongrel,' Chewie seethed. 'I hope he gets what's coming to him.'

'Yeah, bloody oath, Chew,' Ted concurred, trailing off his last syllable, indicating a desire to want to change the subject.

'So, I've got some tips today. You blokes wanna have a punt?'

'A little syndicate would be fun,' Bewsy agreed.

'Chew, you gonna be allowed?' Pilks questioned drolly.

'I've got cash.' Chewie winked. 'Should be sweet.'

The boys laughed, knowing how tight of a rein that his wife kept on their finances.

'What you reckon, Jacko?' Ted asked. 'Maybe win some cash back that the cockhead stole from us?'

I nodded blankly, unenthusiastic about the betting but enjoying the company and break from my mental rambling.

'At least lunch is sorted if we go broke,' Bewsy joked.

The day proceeded from there as we watched the races, with them cheering animatedly at the screen for some and then fervently cursing at the unsuccessful horses for others. The blatantly crestfallen ghost that haunted the house sat amongst them on the couch, occasionally answering their questions with minimal words or pretending to be half-interested in whatever they were discussing.

It wasn't like I was suppressing any form of positive emotion; it was just that I didn't have any. There was nothing, the tank was bone dry. And I just wasn't ready to fully participate in life or be happy; not one ounce of happiness or joy seemed to reside within me.

Dennis joined us in the early evening, armed with a contrite look and a comforting tap on the shoulder. While Royce arrived just before the footy started, with pizza boxes in hand and a similar look as he ruffled my hair.

They both knew the drill; there was no need for redundant questions or grand gestures. Just a seemingly subtle display of care and support was all that was required to show that we were brothers in arms. We all watched the footy together for the remainder of the evening as the boys tried their hardest to brighten the mood and nurse me through the emotional turmoil that I was facing. I really appreciated having them around and couldn't have been more thankful, despite the fact that I didn't contribute as I normally would have. Ted departed us at half-time, while Dennis and Royce left at the end of the footy, as they all had work to attend to in the morning. My other comrades remained with me in our fortress of depressing solitude for another evening, which I was pleased with, given that I wasn't ready to be alone just yet. Eventually, I decided that it was time to confront the possibility of sleep and stood to bid farewell to the remaining occupants of my lounge room. I entered my room huddled in my doona, for another night of probable restlessness.

Chapter 21
A Movie Script Ending

The very next day, I found myself seated in the lounge room in an almost identical position to the day before. I was once again concealed in the depths of the doona that I had draped over myself while the boys rowdily cooked up an elaborate breakfast in the kitchen. The aroma of toast, coffee, bacon, eggs and sausages all combined to scent the room in a pleasant redolence.

After consuming all that we could, the boys and I sluggishly found our way back to the lounge and allowed our food to digest. The dining table sat messily decorated in leftovers that festered in the open air. While the kitchen was clumsily shrouded with soiled pots and pans that were stacked on the counter and in the sink. An apt representation of my life, really. I still wasn't anywhere close to being well; however, I was eating and interacting more and had seemingly begun the painstakingly lengthy process of creeping closer to a more normal disposition.. I still didn't think that I would ever actually reach that destination; it felt like an impossible task, like driving the Nullarbor on a push bike with a flat tyre. But only time would tell, and I considered nothing impossible in my life, given that the seemingly unfeasible had become a curt reality over the past week.

There was a firm knock at the door, interrupting the gentle hum of the television that was playing an old football match. It had been a source of entertainment for the boys, but more importantly for me, a minor distraction from the mental burden that I was inundated with. We all glanced at one another, conjecturing silently as to whom the source of the knock could be and which one of us would be the one of us to heed its call. There hadn't been an expectation of company, nor was I in the mood for any form of conversation with an individual who did not subsist in the current bubble. I shook my head to indicate that the appropriate action was ignorance of the visitor. The boys stared back at me in a hush and after a moment of quiet, the knock was heard again with similar gusto as before.

'Mr Newton, it's Detective West,' came a muffled announcement from the front door that travelled down the hallway and into the living room. 'I need to speak with you.'

I sighed and threw my head back in annoyance, receiving a figurative slap in the face from a gruff reality. The last thing that I wanted to re-hatch was this aspect of my shattered life, but evidently, it had come to deal with me, apparently tiresome of my avoidance of its existence entirely. My mind had been so preoccupied that I had barely given any thought to the other form of chaos that had been brewing previously. The others, who were well-versed in my life's dire situation before the girls' passing, sat still as I relented after the announcement.

'Righto, mate, give me a sec.' I removed the doona that I had draped over me and slowly got to my feet.

I walked down the corridor and opened the door to see Detective West, with his slicked dark brown hair and neat appearance. He gazed at me with his usual stoic countenance. I contrasted him with my tousled exterior, dressed in an old t-shirt and tracksuit pants, with scruffy hair and an unkempt facial fuzz that messily decorated a withered face.

'G'day, Jack,' he said softly. 'How you going, mate?'

I shrugged, my face not changing from its dreary display.

'I understand. May I come in? I have something to inform you about regarding the case.'

I nodded unenthusiastically and let him in. We walked into the lounge room where the others were seated. They greeted the detective politely as I took my seat back on the couch and re-joined the comfort of the doona. I gestured to the detective to procure a chair with the movement of my arm in the direction of the dining table; I had no desire to engage in the formalities of sitting there as we had done previously. The detective obliged, obtaining one and moving it back to the lounge room before beginning in a softer tone than normal after he took his seat.

'I'm sorry to disturb you, Jack. I know you've had a lot on your plate and I'm so sorry about everything that has happened, mate. But we've had a major development in the case and I couldn't get a hold of you on your phone. I wasn't actually sure if you'd be here or not so I just came on a bit of a whim. Anyway, could we have a word in private?'

'Mate, I'm happy for these blokes to hear,' I muttered after I had thought about his request for a moment. 'They pretty much know everything anyway.'

'Okay, that's fair enough,' the detective replied. 'So, have you had any trouble here?'

I paused, letting out a reluctant sigh. 'Nah, I haven't, but in all honesty, I don't really care right now if they come and kill me or not.'

'I understand,' he replied as he nodded unfalteringly, unmoved by the frankness of my speech. 'Anyway, what I need to tell you is that early this morning in a house in Port Moresby, a Mr George Fullarton and a Mrs Elaine Fullarton were found dead. It appears that they were gunned down by someone and we suspect, but can't confirm yet, that it was the bikies that they owed money to.'

The detective studied me carefully. The three boys turned to stare at me in stunned silence, wide-eyed with gaping mouths that conveyed their shock. I didn't react for a while as I let the words wash over me, staring vacantly in the vague direction of the detective's revelation. I hadn't thought about my disdain for those people in what felt like a long while. I didn't feel pleased that they were dead but there was a possible light sense of exoneration. I wasn't sad but felt a slight sense of sympathy for the awful way that they had probably met their end. Ultimately, I knew that this news would not improve my world in the slightest, which was possibly the reason for my lack of emotion.

'Well, I s'pose they got what was coming to them, I dunno,' I muttered eventually.

'It would seem that way,' Detective West responded. 'Now we just need to see if we can get the money back.'

I shrugged and nodded impassively, still searching for emotion.

'Alright, well, I'll leave you all to it,' the detective announced in his usual abrupt refusal to linger.

He stood from his chair and moved it back into its original position before making his way over to me and placing his hand on my shoulder sympathetically.

'All the best, Jack.'

He then politely farewelled the remaining inhabitants of the lounge room and departed promptly, the door snapping shut behind him. The boys all looked at me searchingly, trying to survey the situation silently and gauge my reaction to it.

'You alright, Jacko?' Pilks eventually asked.

'Yeah.'

'How do you feel about it?' Bewsy then quizzed.

'I dunno, mate. Sorta nothing right now.'

'Fuck 'em, Jacko!' Chewie said defiantly. 'They got theirs.'

'I might feel something later but now I'm neither here nor there about it, if I'm honest.'

'Yeah, that's fair enough,' Bewsy responded.

'I don't reckon there's a way you should feel about it,' Pilks concluded. 'Whatever comes, comes.'

I gave a slight nod and then paused for a moment.

'Thanks, boys,' I whispered, subtly indicating my lack of yearning to continue any form of discussion in regard to the matter.

Thankfully, the boys were receptive to my hint and the day continued on as it had been before the detective's bombshell, with the news not mentioned again.

The night also proceeded much in the same way as the previous one, with Royce and Dennis coming over to watch the football. They arrived together, one with dinner in hand and the other with a slab of beer.

'Hello, mate,' Royce soothed as he patted my head.

I glanced up at him and returned a grateful look, while Dennis followed behind him and moved his hand to squeeze my neck comfortingly.

'G'day, Jacko,' he said gently, staring down at me. 'Looking better, mate.'

'Thanks,' I replied quietly, peering up.

He nodded knowingly and then made his way to the kitchen table to gather some chairs for the new arrivals to sit on in the lounge room.

'What's on the menu tonight?' Pilks yelled to the kitchen where Royce stood busily removing the food containers from a plastic bag and organising some bowls for the hungry crowd to use.

'Thai tonight, boys,' Royce announced. 'Smells bloody delicious!'

'Perfect!' Pilks made his way into the kitchen to get his fill, with the rest of the boys quickly following the aroma of the food.

'Come on, Jacko.' Chewie left his seat. 'Let's get something to eat before all these fat cunts eat it all.'

I left the haven of the couch and went over to the kitchen counter where the frenzied activity of adding food to bowls had begun. The boys danced around in an organised chaos to pile their bowls high, while I stood back and watched, waiting for them to finish their turns.

'Anyone got any bets on tonight?' asked Bewsy. 'Might be fun to have a little punt, hey?' Bewsy looked at me hopefully, endeavouring to gauge the success of his attempted morale booster.

I gave a half smile and nodded in agreeance.

'Yep, keen as mustard for that,' Dennis responded as he made his way back to his seat in the lounge room to join Royce.

'Nothing wrong with a bit of money in the old skyrocket to start the weekend!' Royce added.

'Ah, beauty, the boys aren't here to fuck spiders, that's for sure,' Bewsy said jokingly. 'Chew, the misso gonna let you have a punt two days in a row?'

'She won't, but we'll try and keep this one quiet somehow,' Chewie replied as he winked at me cheekily, with the boys in the room chortling at his response.

'Chew, you're a legend in your own lunch box, mate!' Pilks jeered.

'This is married life, John,' Chewie remarked. 'It's a battle to keep little secrets and tell white lies. You would know if you actually had the plums to get married!'

The room once again laughed in chorus as the boys continued to heckle each other flippantly. I eventually made up my plate and joined everyone in the lounge, taking my regular seat on the couch as the boys hungrily devoured their food in a lull.

'You blokes hear about George and Elaine?' I muttered after a while.

Dennis looked up at me and shook his head.

'Nah, what?' Royce said as he stopped eating and looked at me intently.

'Dead,' I said dryly.

They both gawked at me.

'Get fucked!' Royce cried.

'You're kidding!' Dennis replied. 'How? Who told you?'

'The detective came round and told us today,' I responded. 'Apparently they were gunned down.'

'Jesus!' Royce remarked, appearing stunned.

'Christ, mate,' Dennis spluttered. 'How do you feel about that?

'Not much.' I shrugged. 'Still impartial about it.'

No one spoke or ate for a moment.

'Oh well, good riddance,' Bewsy eventually stated. 'Bad way to die but bit of karma really, isn't it?'

'Yeah, can't say I feel too sorry for them,' Royce said.

We all nodded as we reconvened our eating.

'It's a toughie, really, to know how to feel about it,' Pilks added.

'Nah, you heard me before,' Chewie reminded. 'Fuck 'em.'

'You sure you're alright, Jacko?' Dennis inquired.

'Yeah, with that, I'm honestly fine,' I replied. 'Bit of closure, if anything, I s'pose.'

'Still a shock, though,' Royce said.

'Yeah, it is,' I responded weakly.

'Okay, enough about those knobs,' Bewsy proclaimed. 'Let's get a multi or something happening.'

'Alright, I'll do it on my phone,' announced Royce. 'How much we thinking?'

'Twenty each?' asked Dennis.

'Yep, twenty is good,' agreed Chewie. 'I can talk my way out of twenty bucks coming out of the joint account!'

The boys all cackled, while I gave a half-hearted snort to resemble a laugh.

'Okay boys, transfer twenty sheets to me then, please,' Royce requested. 'Jacko, I'll cover you.'

I looked up at him and bowed my head appreciatively.

'What we gonna bet on?' Pilks quizzed.

'Not first goal scorer or anything like that,' Bewsy suggested. 'Then you're out of your multi before you know it!'

'Listen to the master,' Royce said waggishly. 'I'll sort us out, had a few wins this season.'

'Yep, I reckon you're the man for the job, Roycey,' concurred Dennis. 'I've got no bloody clue about this stuff.'

We all watched the footy together that evening, embroiled in the fickle cultural pastime of sports gambling, which proved victorious in the end and multiplied everyone's twenty-dollar contribution into a reasonably generous return. Personally, I spent the night still torn between sympathy and satisfaction at the outcome of George and Elaine's grisly end, which at the very least, had provided a partial distraction from the true source of my mind's unrest. At the footy's conclusion, I bid the boys farewell as I gathered my doona and made my way to my bedroom. I was completely exhausted from the cerebral acrobatics that had proceeded the day's revelations. Plus, the previous night's sleep had been completely sporadic in nature. As I got to my bedroom door, I stopped and turned to look back at them all.

'Boys, I really appreciate everything you've all done for me these past couple of days but I think I'm ready to deal with this all by myself now,' I announced. 'You need to get on with your lives and I need to get on with mine.'

They all nodded understandingly as I turned and went to bed.

VIII.

I miss you like the desire for light on a gloomy day,

like the soft caress of an ocean wave.

I miss you like the wintry lust for the warmth of sun,

like without you, I don't know what I will become.

Chapter 22
The Ghost of You

The next morning greeted me with its accustomed dreary gloom, which hit me harder than usual because of the fact that I had farewelled my comrades the night before. I had mainly done it for them, even though they had been a pleasant distraction and a shelter from the harrowing loneliness. For one, the fact that I had sent them away of my own accord meant that they could go home to their partners and conduct their normal lives without the guilt of leaving me alone; while secondly, I felt that I needed to deal with my problems personally, without the aid of others. It was the right thing, for all of us.

I lay in bed and contemplated what I wanted to fill my day with. I still had no strength to partake in normal life, hindered by a defiant sorrow to wallow in and a lack of desire to fight it. This was when the thought of actively using alcohol to numb the pain was displayed in my mind and I began to internally deliberate on its merits. I knew that I was stronger than my father had been and therefore able to avoid addiction to this method of coping. Plus, the attraction of anaesthetisation, coupled with the alteration of time that alcohol could provide when sharing in its consumption, was hard to pass up. Therefore, I decided that a journey to the bottle-o was necessitated and got up to dress in more appropriate attire.

Entering the lounge was strange, I had half-expected for the boys to be on the couch, but all that I was confronted with was an eerie quietness. Outside, the world was an outlandish concept for someone who had withdrawn. I squinted with the glary light that shone through the dim clouds, electing to make the short journey to the bottle shop on foot. Luckily, Bruce was nowhere to be seen as I darted past his place without detection, having no desire to share in any political commentary or inappropriate jokes. The light grew murkier during my travels, the sunlight swallowed by darker clouds that grew in visual threat, along with an increased wind gust. Eventually, I was confronted by the busyness of cars and the chime of trams as they jostled for space out the front of the strip of shops that lined the endlessly long main road. I entered the bright, well-lit store to the greeting of the attendant, becoming immediately aware of an even more frigid temperature inside as I ventured to the spirits section. I wanted my liquor black, like my life; like my heart and soul. I scanned the shelves until I found the scotch, picking up the biggest bottle that they had. As I approached the counter, I had a sudden compulsion to get cigarettes too, which I requested from the attendant; a whim of self-destructive tendency or a boredom filler, I wasn't sure. Speckles of light rain spat from the gloomy sky as I departed the shop, which hastened my journey back to the quieter streetscape and fortitude of home.

After returning from my reacquaintance with the outside world, I went about shielding the house, closing all of the blinds in the lounge room and kitchen to create a visual darkness. I wanted it to be a dark and dismal habitat where a creature with feelings like the ones that resided in me would belong. I poured the scotch straight into a glass, with the addition of only ice cubes. I wished for it to burn a little, possibly to make me feel another discomfort other than emotional pain. I then lit a cigarette and inhaled, it too burned with an irritation that was combined with comforting warmth. I puffed the smoke out into the empty room.

Wrapped in my familiar doona and surrounded by darkness, I lay on the couch and drank in the poison, observing the masculine familial vocation of drinking to self-medicate when infected with grief and pity. I had accepted it all; I knew that I wasn't going to be able to crawl out of the abyss at that instant, and truthfully, I wasn't even willing to try. I turned on the television and let it entertain itself, which provided some relief from the silence, as I let my mind wander to wherever it aspired to go. Occasionally, I would snap back into coherence and become aware of the picture that the television provided, but for the most part, I became lost in the depths of my mind. A sip of dark liquor would slide down my throat and enter my bloodstream with its numbing agents, providing me with placation and comfort, like a potion that had the power to ease my grief minutely with every sip. And a tiny ease in grief was better than none at all. It warmed the inside of a being who had previously felt lifeless and cold; a being who had a heart that he felt was broken and a soul that he felt had died when his girls had left him. It provided me with a sense that I could still experience a form of tenderness within me. It was a sort of warm embrace that damaged people seek, like a drunken regular at the local pub who pursues tenderness from alcohol to help them to combat all of the plaguing hardships that they have faced in their life. It was probably what my father, James Newton, was seeking when he lost his wife and began to neglect his son; warmth and an elixir that would help him to forget. I finally understood him. I was in the same abyss that he had plunged into after Mum's death. And if a person didn't have the grit to drag themselves out, then they simply wouldn't. And he obviously didn't; he just chose to wallow and create a life around it.

The rainy day passed in a smoky haze and alcoholic blur. Eventually my deep meditations were interrupted by a panicky knock at the door, which snapped me back into reality.

'Jacko, it's Dennis!' came a voice on the front veranda.

I finished the remaining contents of my glass of scotch and begrudgingly left my isolation to make my way to the door, opening it to discover a man who looked like he'd seen a ghost.

He was not the comforting or sympathetic man that I had expected to see; he was stiff and fearful, with a daunted and unnerved disposition. Dennis entered the dingy lair without a word and made his way into the lounge area. He spotted the bottle of scotch on the floor next to the cigarettes and a makeshift ashtray and immediately moved into the kitchen to attain a glass of his own. He progressed to the single-seater, where he began shakily pouring himself a scotch. His hands trembled and he held himself in an uncharacteristically edgy manner before taking a large gulp of his drink. I watched all of his movements from the couch, studying him curiously. His face glowed weakly with the vague radiance of the television, which was the only source of light in the cheerlessly dark enclosure, adding to the weirdness of the moment.

'You okay?' I asked puzzledly.

'I resigned,' Dennis eventually stammered as he looked at me nervously. 'I just can't do it anymore.'

'What!? Why?' I asked, stunned by his reply.

Upon consideration of my question, he proceeded to skull his remaining scotch with one large gulp. He winced and wiped his mouth with a groan, before he picked up the bottle and began to pour himself another. I continued to watch him closely, still completely astonished by his uncouth behaviour.

'Look, Jacko, I gotta tell you something.' He sighed heavily. 'But I just don't know how to say it.'

My mind raced. *What possible news could give him such an astoundingly peculiar countenance?* A nervousness grew and my heart drummed faster as I struggled to find the words to say. The part of my brain that was responsible for speech was either drowned in alcohol or held hostage by the bustle of my mind's curiosity.

'Just tell me, mate,' I said, attempting to purvey a tranquil manner in order to appease Dennis.

Again, he took a large gulp of his drink and grimaced as he swallowed. He exhaled loudly, his eyes flickering hesitantly as if he was scrambling for the right words to say.

'Okay, well...' he mumbled. 'So today at the station...'

He paused again, squirming in his chair as he moved the glass to his mouth with a shaky hand and proceeded to finish his drink. I continued to gaze at him, barely moving a muscle, spellbound in nervous anticipation as his eyes moved about in an attempt to avoid my gaze.

'Well, an officer came to me today at the station, who had worked on the girls'... case. She... she was at the – uhh – the scene.'

He left his chair and stood tensely before walking over to the kitchen counter on the other side of the room to lean on it and recommence his sentence.

'Anyway, when she had first arrived on the scene, they had noticed two sets of tire marks before the break in the barrier where the car had – ahhh – left the road.'

I pulled the doona tighter and hugged myself consolingly. There had not been one mention of the incident since it had occurred. The reference to it distressed me, despite the fact that I had combed over the event so many times in my mind.

'So apparently, on the side of the car, there were some white scratch marks that indicated—'

I became agitated with him as a fearful tingle resonated throughout my body.

'What, Dennis?' I yelled impatiently. 'For fuck's sake, just tell me, mate!'

'It wasn't an accident,' he blurted. 'Someone ran them off the road deliberately.'

I recoiled in horror. The weight of the words hit me with an immense force. The world spun nauseously. An icy burn coursed through my veins as tears welled in my eyes. Dennis moved back to the couch to put his hand on my shoulder to comfort me.

'Jacko, I'm so sorry, mate, but there's more,' he said, with a pained expression.

His nervous disposition had faded slightly after his revelation, appearing to be superseded by his concern. I began to sob in disbelief that someone could have killed my innocent family; I felt so ill with the guilt of not being able to protect them.

'So, they were there at the accident, conducting an investigation, when the police chief rocked up to the site. He immediately shut down the investigation and told them that there was no need to conduct any further investigations because it was a simple car accident caused by a careless driver.'

He rested for a moment and took a deep breath while I continued to cry with his hand on my shoulder.

'Anyway, the female constable who was at the scene got wind that earlier that day there had been a report of a stolen white-coloured car not too far from the crash site. So, she dug a little deeper and found out the stolen car was registered to an address that was near a street called Cornwall Street, I think. Anyway, this street name rang a bell because it was where she had been a few times for disturbances or inquiries to a house that a known standover man for a bikie gang lived...'

I immediately stopped my sobbing after this disclosure. The blow of the words took my breath from me. I looked at Dennis, aghast; my whole body shook viciously.

'You think the bikie who came to see me killed them?' I choked.

'I think it's very possible,' Dennis whispered after taking a deep breath, 'and the corrupt bastards that I worked for have covered it up.'

An intense rage bubbled in me; it was white hot and it coursed through every blood vessel in my body. My blood boiled with fury. My muscles tensed, breathing became audibly weighted. I let out an almighty scream before picking up my glass and throwing it hard against the wall.

I leapt from the couch and made my way to the kitchen table, scalding with an uncontrollable wrath that I had never felt before. I picked up the table and flipped it, letting out a guttural howl as it came crashing to the floor. I hurled the chairs across the room in the direction of the back door and windows, shattering them with violent blows. Shards of glass spewed across the floor. The ferocity within me remained unextinguished. I moved to the wall and punched through the plaster with my fists repeatedly; no pain was felt.

Dennis tackled me to the ground. He gripped me tightly in an effort to curtail me, much like he had undoubtedly done to the many criminals that he'd tussled with in the line of duty. I attempted to resist but my strength faded rapidly along with my anger. I began to cry loudly, inundated with the persistent sadness that had returned.

'I know, mate, I know,' Dennis soothed. 'Let it all out.'

He released his grasp on me after a while when he realised that my rage had been quelled. Tears flowed, dousing the ireful temper that had come before them. I contemplated staying put and waiting there until life had left my grief-stricken body. I was hollow enough, I felt that it wouldn't take very long. *Can I even go on with existence, fully aware that the two most precious people in my life had met their ends by cold-blooded murder?* I hated myself for feeling even the slightest bit of sympathy for George and Elaine's deaths and hoped that they had suffered during their murder; if there was a hell, I genuinely hoped that they were going to burn in it for eternity.

Dennis and I lay on the floor for ages, like two people lying supine in deep reflection on a field, staring at a star-speckled night sky. Except our field had floorboards and shattered glass, our sky was starless and shrouded in the darkness of the night outside. Only the soft glow of the telly provided an iridescence to our surroundings. The setting represented my universe; my cosmos had no stars anymore and was just a dark nothingness, while my planet had lost its mother star to orbit around and existed in a perpetual darkness. It was during this darkened meditation that the memory of my dream flashed in my mind. I saw Matilda and Helena. I saw Helena's supple lips mouthing the only words that she had said: 'Everything is not as it seems.'

I lay in a silent astonishment; the words made sense.

'What should I do?' I eventually muttered to break the hush, holding my gaze at the nothingness of the ceiling.

Dennis breathed in audibly through his nose and sighed. He knew exactly what I meant by my question. I was really asking: *'Should I try and kill this bastard?'*

'Look, mate,' he began quietly, keeping his stare at the black ceiling as well. 'I've never suffered a loss like you but I deal with situations like this all the time. You're gonna want to do some pretty irrational things right now. But my advice to you is to just please think about it. We can fight this together.'

'I just feel so hopeless and angry. My heart is so broken. I don't know what I should do,' I whispered painfully.

'I know, mate,' Dennis returned solemnly. 'I can only imagine what you're feeling. But please promise me that we'll work things out together. We always have.'

I paused for a moment before responding.

'Alright,' I uttered. 'We'll do it together.'

'Good, mate,' he responded.

We lay for a while longer in a quiet stillness as we contemplated things. The gentle hum of the television, along with the chime of cicadas that blew in with a soft draught through the jaggedly open windows, filled the elongated taciturnity.

'I've been thinking about reconciling with Dad,' I eventually whispered.

'Really?' Dennis responded quietly. 'How come?'

'Now that I know what he went through, it's made me understand how someone could get to the state that he got to. I was actually considering going to his place before you got here. I really think I wanna do it. Do you reckon you could give me a lift there now?'

'Ah, yeah, mate, if that's what you want. I can take you there,' he uttered, sounding surprised.

Dennis got to his feet and helped me to mine as we dusted ourselves off and made our way out to his car. The night was briskly still. It felt as if something ominous was soon to arrive to the surprise of an unexpectant recipient; it felt as though revenge lingered in the air. Little did Dennis know, during my time on the floor I had remembered that Dad kept a pistol at his house. In truth, I had no intentions of reconciling with that man. It appeared that everything was not as it seemed at all.

IX.

Inside me there lurks an evil,

born and bred from love's upheaval.

A darkness in my bones it hides,

a darkness in my heart it resides.

What am I to do with this rage,

am I to restraint it in its cage?

Or should I do what my heart intends,

and gain myself a sweet revenge?

Chapter 23
You've Haunted Me All My Life

The night was dark as we drove. The only source of light apart from Dennis' dim headlights was the fleeting orange glow of streetlamps as we passed them. Few words were spoken; Dennis probably thought that the reason for the muteness was because I was nervous about reconciling with my dad, but it wasn't at all. I sat there, stiff as a board, my jaw clenched tightly along with my fists. My body felt hard, bulletproof almost, like I could take on an army and not have a scratch on me after I had defeated them.

My depression was now a distant companion, overtaken by the rage that resided within me. I wanted revenge. I wanted suffering. I wanted death as a method of appeasement. A bloodlust swirled. I had never felt this overwhelming sensation before – it was the most engulfing rage; the most intoxicating fury; the most devastating anger. My boiling blood was like lava coursing through my body. It ran hot through my blood vessels, passing on the bloodlust to every cell in my being and advising them to be prepared for carnage. My heart drummed in my chest, so hard and loud that I could hear it in my ears – in fact, I was surprised that Dennis couldn't hear it for himself. It was like a huge jungle drum being pounded by an Amazon tribesman in the depths of the wilderness. The tense car fogged while we drove. I let the windows down slightly to allow some cold air through the small gap to cool my silent rage.

'A bit nervous, mate?' Dennis asked.

'Yeah, a bit.' I nodded with a deep breath.

We rounded the corner into Somerset Street, the setting for my childhood and bittersweet adolescence. It was the street where I had learnt to ride a bike and spent endless summers playing cricket or footy with the other kids that had lived there. It was the street that had housed Mum's cancer battle and the place where I had lost the man that I had known as my father. It was the street where, many years ago, I had closed the front door to the house and desired to never return. But here I was. And the reason for my return was the most bewildering part.

'Okay. Good luck, Jacko,' Dennis said as he pulled up outside the front of the house. 'Do you want me to hang around?'

I looked at him. He had a comforting half-smile on his face in an attempt to provide reassurance to his nervous counterpart.

'No, all good, mate,' I said in response with a nod before leaving the car. 'Thanks, legend. For everything.'

As Dennis drove off down the street, I turned to survey the house in front of me. Its white weatherboards were cracked and peeling, revealing a greyed timber, either as a result of sun exposure or anguish – I couldn't be sure. It was once such a sanctuary of love and safety; now, it looked haunted and exuded heartache. It was painted in pain and suffering. The windows showed no evidence of life inside, as the ghost that dwelled within its walls was most likely engaged in a heavy slumber after a day of alcohol consumption.

I made my way around to the laneway that ran by the back of the house. Its wooden boundary fence was dilapidated and stood slightly taller than my head. I held the top of it with both hands and hoisted myself up, just enough to be able to extend my arms and rest on the fence for a moment in order to view the backyard. It presented as I had anticipated: wildly overgrown and unkempt. A prominently wild lawn of knee-high grass and weeds shrouded most of the yard, with a thick border of disorderly bushes that grew around the majority of the perimeter. A gap was formed in the perimeter's shrubbery to allow off-street parking onto a small paved area in the back corner of the block. Just beyond the paving was a timber shed, which had been the resting place of the gun when I had lived there, and I dearly hoped at that instant that the hiding spot had remained unchanged.

After this momentary glance to envisage a clear passage, I pulled my legs up and planted my feet on the top of the fence before leaping onto the paved surface. I stuck the landing reasonably quietly and then crept to the shed, much like a cat burglar slinks through a location en route to an item that they wish to steal. I carefully opened the door, which was seldom locked, as Dad had always hated the concept of inconvenience to entering his own shed. Sliding into the opening, I turned to view the area; a small, dark room that smelt quite musty, like a combination of wet clothes, detergent and an earthy rust. A small window allowed a tiny amount of moonlight into the room. It dully lit a busy bench that ran along the entire wall at about waist height. It was littered with a haphazard array of plastic containers, glass jars and small boxes, which contained what appeared to be every screw, bolt and plastic thingamajig known to mankind.

The wall was adorned with a collection of various rusty tools that hung from hooks, while under the bench was a mower that had obviously gone unused for a while, given the backyard's current dishevelment. On the bench in the furthest corner, covered by the messy array of bric-a-brac, I uncovered the grey metallic box that I had expected to find. It was just large enough to accommodate the pistol that it usually retained. A coded lock on its face stared back at me, glistening slightly in the moonlight. Luckily, I could recall the rudimentary combination quite easily, given it was the date of my mother's birthday. I entered the code and the lock popped open. I lifted the lid of the small box and gazed inside. To my dismay, the gun was nowhere to be seen.

'It's not there anymore, mate,' came a raspy voice from behind me.

It startled me slightly, but with the voice came a recognition of familiarity. I turned to view its source. There he was, my dad, standing out the front of the shed's partially-opened door, only slightly visible in the shadowiness. He opened the door wide and switched on the light of the shed, which flashed brightly a few times, giving me slight glimpses of his true form before eventually illuminating the area permanently.

I stood silently and wide-eyed; this was a man that I hadn't laid my eyes on in over a decade. His figure contained recognisable features that time and alcoholic misuse had warped. His pale face was dry and withered, covered in parts by scruffy, unkempt facial hair and clusters of spider veins that gathered on his puffy cheeks and purplish nose. His brown, defeated eyes were decorated with large bags under them; his forehead was wrinkled and arid, cracked like sun-scorched earth that one would find in the desert. His short hair was grubbily ragged, mostly black like mine, but in some parts, it was dusted with grey speckles. A large belly protruded through his stained blue singlet, although the rest of his body appeared to show evidence of a once-athletic physique.

'Where is it?' I stuttered.

'I moved it inside,' he replied. 'I realised how bloody stupid it was to keep it in the shed.'

We both paused for a moment, conjecturing on what to say.

'Dad, I need it,' I muttered.

'Now, what the bloody hell would you need that gun for?' he responded with a calm curiosity.

I hesitated, wondering how much of the story I needed to tell him and how much of the story he already knew.

'The girls are dead.'

He sighed loudly. 'Yeah, I know. I'm so sorry, mate. I came to the chapel but you didn't seem like you were in the mood for talking.'

I looked at him and nodded blankly. He paused, looking mildly confused.

'What do you want the gun for, then?'

I hesitated slightly before responding. 'Someone killed them.'

His glassy eyes flashed in astonishment. 'How do you know that?'

'I just do.'

'And you want to avenge them with my gun?'

I vacantly nodded as he stood and thought, exhaling loudly in the process.

'Look, I know I haven't been a great father, or even a father to you at all, but let me say one thing. Humans are primitive beasts deep down and there is most likely no God who created us. So, who do we answer to when all is said and done? We answer to ourselves and ourselves only. You need to do whatever appeases your soul. I s'pose what I'm trying to say is that I get it, mate. I understand what you wanna do and I'm not gonna stop you.'

I stood in quiet awe, attempting to decipher these partially drunken, yet inciteful ramblings. It was apparent that an admirable intelligence still frustratingly resided somewhere deep within him.

'Wait here,' he instructed as he left for the inside of the house.

I meditated on the last part of his ramble; he made a lot of sense. When all was said and done, I only had myself to answer to. I needed to do this for my soul. I couldn't live my life knowing that my girls had suffered while the cretin who had killed them had been allowed to live their life uninhibited. It didn't seem just to me. At that very moment, I knew exactly what needed to be done. After a while, my father returned, gripping the pistol by its barrel in one hand and holding some jingling keys in the other.

'Here you go, mate,' he said as he handed me the gun. 'She's ready to go.'

I returned a grateful nod, in mild disbelief that he was simply handing the gun to me. He then dropped his car keys into my free hand.

'I saw that someone dropped you off. Take my car. Revenge is quicker that way.'

Again, I shot him another look of incredulity with a bow of my head as we both moved out of the shed. I felt the sudden urge to hug him and I could tell that he felt the same way.

'Take care of yourself, Dad,' I whispered as we exchanged a brief embrace in the gloomy moonlight.

'You too, Jack.'

I made my way to the back gate and pulled up the rusty latch on one of its doors to partially open it. Before I exited, I turned to see my dad staring at me from the shadows of the backyard, the murky light of the night sky had made him look as if he was standing in the part of the abyss that he had built a life in. It made me feel as if I was watching him fade into oblivion. For all I knew, he may have been thinking the very same thing.

Chapter 24
No Pity nor Fear

I sprinted down the alleyway and back into the street where my father's car sat out the front of the house. It was an old white Holden Commodore, a rust bucket in fact, littered with old form guides and takeaway food packaging on the inside. This signified all that it was used for, split between adventures to the local pub to have a bet at the tote and journeys for fast food. The door creaked loudly as I opened it and got in, greeted with a musty staleness that was ingrained into it – a mixture of greasy alcohol and decaying ink on paper.

I sped away in a bloodthirsty pursuit as the antiquated vehicle groaned in response, its neglected engine choking to lug me to my destination. I was familiar with the Cornwall Street that Dennis had mentioned when he had divulged the unpleasant news to me; it was only a short journey around the corner from the infamous Rocco Falcone. The car fogged as my heart pumped sweltering blood around my body. Sorrow and rage had combined to burst in a violent eruption, engulfing me like lava sweeping through innocent villages during a volcanic explosion.

My hands tightly gripped the steering wheel as I drove rapidly. My mind ticked over, many questions swirled, most of them without definite answers. I wondered how killing someone would feel. *Would I actually be able to go through with it if I had the chance?* It all felt entirely possible. I was fuelled by an extreme rage that filled me with a steeliness – a morosely malevolent ability to be able to achieve feats that I'd never thought was possible of a compassionately peaceful human being such as myself.

After a short while, only moments of presence, in fact, I arrived at Cornwall Street. It was a dim thoroughfare, lit by weak streetlight and a small crescent moon with its neighbouring scattering of stars. The streetscape was quietly still and showed minimal evidence of life, apart from the dull glow of inside lights from neighbouring houses that were mostly obscured by curtains. I decided that the best method was to drive down the street and gauge whether any house displayed evidence of a bikie occupation, although I didn't exactly know what that meant.

I slowed my driving pace to a crawl, moving my head methodically from left to right to try and determine a house that fit my vague ideals. Most of the houses were pleasantly neat. They looked like cheerful places that housed adoring families, who would most likely be nestled together in front of the television or around the dinner table, excitedly talking about their days as others listened lovingly. None of them fit my mental description of somewhere that would be capable of housing a murderer.

I had almost neared the end of the long street when I spotted a dwelling that caught my eye; it looked slightly out of place compared to the rest of the homes, with an untidy front yard and scruffily dishevelled house behind it. The grass was high in parts, while in another part there was no growth at all, leading to the inference that sunlight had been obscured from contact with the lawn to prevent it from photosynthesising. The space was smaller than a car would leave and I speculated for a minute as to whether a motorbike could have been left there for an extended period.

I parked the car a few houses up and got out. The briskly cold air hit my warm skin as I stood and looked around the street to see if anybody was about. The coast was clear. I quietly closed the door and obscured the gun that I was holding in the loose pocket of my pants, creeping over to the edge of the property. I studied the red-bricked house, which contained a plain concrete driveway that housed two old cars and led to a decrepit carport. Its front weatherboard porch was decaying and askew to one side, with paint peeling from its rotten timber, indicating a complete lack of house pride or care from its inhabitant. The driveway provided a clear and unobscured passage along the fence line by the side of the cars. I quickly determined that there was no form of sensor light on the carport or house that would flash to unveil an intruder such as myself.

I slunk by the far side of the first car and into the gap afforded between the two sedans. From there, I could see into the large front window of the house that was closest to me. It showed the glow of a television that illuminated a stocky, bald, middle-aged man, who appeared to be alone. I studied him closely as the light from the screen danced across his hardened face. He wore a black t-shirt and leather vest, with black jeans, and rested his feet up on a coffee table, drinking a can of beer and smoking a cigarette.

I watched him for a moment as I mentally planned my next move, the angle of the television made him face in a direction that prevented him from discovering his stalker in full view. I crept from the gap in the cars to move further along the fence, obscured by the front car as I sneaked, with the gun gripped in my right hand. Under the carport, I discovered a large object in the shadows, which was concealed by a black plastic cover. Cautiously, I removed a small part of the covering to reveal the wheel of a motorbike and ran my index finger over the soft black rubber to confirm.

I stopped for an instant in my crouched position, analysing all of the evidence that I had in front of me. The man inside wore the same clothes and had the same hard-bodied physical aspects that the bikie had embodied. This man had a motorbike, but then again, so did thousands of people who weren't members of a murderous bikie gang. The only discerning feature that I knew was his voice; it was burned in my mind. The gravelly, raspy, threatening voice. A voice of hundreds of stand overs, a voice of fear and inferred pain, a deeply sinister bark. I moved closer to the corner of the window that was safely veiled by the open curtains to further attempt to determine his identity.

His face displayed a permanent scowl as he squinted slightly to watch his television. I surveyed the way that he sipped his beer, the way that he smirked at the television, the way he dragged his cigarette and then obnoxiously exhaled the smoke into the air. I listened intently to any noise in the house, with bated breath, preventing any movement of my body; I could hear the soft murmur of the television and his occasional throaty cough that nestled amongst distant outside noises.

For whatever reason, it was at this precise moment that the wind of fate seemed to blow my way because, in the next instant, a dog detected my presence. It let out a bark from the side gate that was closest to me to advise its owner of unwelcome company. The man's head immediately turned to the window.

'Who the fuck is that?' he yelled as he squinted while trying to make out the origin of the ruckus.

My blood curdled. My heart screamed. The violent rage overtook my whole body once again. That was the voice. It was the voice that had threatened me and it was the voice of the man that had killed my girls. I was sure of it.

I moved to the centre of the window to reveal myself. The man stood up from his chair and laid his eyes on me. He froze as he saw the gun in my hand, his gaze widening in horror. I gripped it tightly as my body pulsed with fury.

I pulled the trigger. I didn't hear the gunshot. It was muted by heavy breathing and the thumping of my heart. The glass window shattered as the bullet pierced through and travelled in the man's direction. He dropped to the ground with a thud. I smashed through the remnants of the window and stormed into the house to stand over him. He lay cowered on the ground with his hands covered in crimson blood that gushed from the bullet wound to his stomach.

The scowl on his face had been replaced with a look of pure devastation. He looked up at me in anguish, struggling to verbalise.

'Why the fuck did you kill my wife and daughter?' I screamed as I held the gun to his face.

'Please, mate,' he stammered in pain. 'I can explain. I'm so sorry. I don't wanna die.'

My steely resolve didn't flinch. My anger had overtaken my ability to feel sympathy or compassion for a debauched reprobate such as him. He looked helpless. *But did he think about my girls when he had killed them? Did he show them any compassion or feel any remorse?* It was highly doubtful.

'Start fucking talking!' I shouted.

'It wasn't for us,' he spluttered. 'It was for Rocco Falcone. He wanted them dead! I swear!'

I gasped in horror; I couldn't believe it. A jolt ran through my entire body as I screamed. I screeched in rage, in shock, in terror, in the growth of my desire for a savage revenge. I looked straight at the man as I pointed the gun at his face and pulled the trigger again. His head thudded back to the floor. A cherry-red firework of blood spat back at me, a red river beginning to flow from the bullet hole that appeared in his forehead.

I began to tremble slightly, my body shaking with the realisation that I had actually killed another human being. It felt surreal, dream-like almost, but after a brief moment of weakness, a sudden wave of reassurance and sense of vindication washed over me. I had righted a wrong. It was an eye for an eye and no loss to the world. I snapped back to reality with a sudden epiphany; Rocco Falcone was a dead man.

Chapter 25
To the End

I ran back to the car, quickly started the engine and sped off, wiping the blood splatters from my face with the back of my hand. Everything felt bizarre, as if I was existing in a fantasy, like in the dream world where I'd strangled George. I stewed on an anger that was too overwhelming to be true, while the actions themselves were too unreal for the authentic Jack Newton to have actually performed. But even the most passive man had his limits. This had triggered something deep within me; a malevolence that every innocently non-violent person must have had lurking within them and was only woken from its dormancy in the most extreme of circumstances.

Mine was awoken – it coursed through me, overtaking and propelling me towards the delivery of a sinister fate. I pulled up out the front of the boxy property with its distinctive high fence. The street was lined with cars but not a soul stirred. I left the car and softly closed the door.

Upon studying the presence of security cameras and sensor lights, which were fixed to the outside of the lifeless house, I determined that my best course of action was to gain entry from the rear. I leapt the small front fence of the next-door neighbours, running along the edge of their property before jumping over the side gate and into their backyard, which was thankfully uninhabited by man or beast. I knew the anatomy of Rocco's backyard well, given I had been to his house on a few occasions to discuss his grand renovation plans. I made my way down the fence line until I reached a spot where a lawn existed on the other side. Gripping the fence, I hoisted myself up and leapt onto the small patch of turf in the far corner of his backyard.

I froze in position until I was sure that my presence had gone undetected and there was no one about. The inner torment that resided within me, along with the impending violence that I wished to execute, would have been perfectly signified with violent rain or thunder by a Hollywood director. But the night was mostly still, a sparkling of scattered stars and a partial moon in the dark night sky looked down upon me.

To my right stood the beginnings of Rocco's ill-fated extension, which had grand plans of being a gaudy indoor-outdoor bar that extended from his ostentatious pool room. Unfortunately for him, it only resembled a dismal looking concrete slab, with an upright timber frame emerging from it. The rest of the house was dark, except for a dim illumination that flashed through the grand glass panelling of the upstairs room. It made a dull reflection on the large, rectangular pool in front of me. I knew that the light was him; the bringer of misery and the extinguisher of my light.

I crept stealthily across the backyard to the other side of the house, planned to be the site of an extravagant kitchen and lounge area that opened onto the pool through the most utterly audacious doors that one had ever imagined. The large, empty opening in the timber framing that was intended for the doors, was obscured by a thick plastic sheeting that prevented wind from blowing into the house. It fluttered gently in the chilly air, which broke the stagnant silence of the murky night with its flapping. I held one of the keys to it and began hacking with its jagged edges in an attempt to cut through, until eventually creating an entrance point and prudently making my way into the unfinished space. The whole bottom storey appeared devoid of any form of brightness and showed no signs of life. I looked around with narrowed eyes and tried to make out the contents of the dim room. I was stood on a dusty concrete slab, which had unfulfilled ambitions of being polished, and was surrounded by unplastered timber stud walls, along with a partially assembled kitchen. The soft resonance of a melody drifted from upstairs via the stairwell, along with a lacklustre beam of light. The illumination came from the back room that I had viewed initially from the yard. It was the devil's lair.

I sneaked over to the staircase and gazed up cautiously. I could see the light coming from the end of a hallway at the top of the stairs, accompanied by the more evident sound of classical music. I cringed at how pretentious he was. I removed the gun from my pocket and gripped it tightly with both hands, sidling up the staircase as soundlessly as a church mouse.

My hands trembled in anticipation. My heart thumped loudly once more. I stared carefully down the hallway; the light shone from a pompous room that I had found myself in when we had first begun our renovation plans with Rocco. It hosted a colossal television affixed to the wall, along with an expensive leather couch, a vintage record player and an extraordinary collection of records; while the opposite side was adorned with enormous bookshelves that covered the walls of one half of the room. In front of the bookshelves, which were filled with an impressively monstrous assortment of hard-cover books, was a dark brown, single-seater chesterfield sofa, with an antique side table that sat next to it. This was where Rocco kept an ashtray and box of cigars, along with a decanter of scotch, a tumbler glass and a small lamp to illuminate his haughty endeavours and self-satisfaction. It appeared that the evil creature liked to sit with the company of expensive liquor, hard-cover books and his inflated ego.

I nimbly slunk down the hallway, imperceptibly planting one foot on the carpet in front of the other. I held my breath. The anger in my body built like a storm. Dark clouds engulfed the entire sky of my mind and thrashes of violent lighting and thunder shook in the depths of my soul. I felt like nothing could defeat me.

With the gun fixed to my hand, I clenched my jaw in anticipation of impending vengeance. I entered the room and turned to my right to view the source of the light. It was him.

He looked up immediately, half in surprise and half in expectance, with the aura of a seemingly cool and calm Bond villain. He sat cross-legged in his chair, holding a book in one hand, draped in a maroon silk dressing gown with a gold trim. He'd even had the pretentiousness to have it embroidered with his initials on the breast.

Amongst other items, the side table next to him contained a half-full tumbler of scotch; the room was hazed with cigar smoke, accompanied by the smell of freshly opened books and a leathery mahogany. I stared at him wrathfully, deep into the eyes that gazed back. They looked pitch black; evil and non-human. I had never hated someone in my entire life as much as the man who sat in front of me. My breathing became more frenetic as I raised the gun in his direction. He calmly put his book down on the side table and took a sip of his scotch, swallowing with a small wince. He gave a half smile before holding the tumbler up to me in a seemingly cocky salute.

'Well, if you're going to die, you might as well have a sip of the good stuff before you go,' he announced coolly, in a mockingly confident manner. 'Don't you think?'

I tingled with an icy sweat that graced my skin, mitigating the steam that felt like it was rising from my pores.

'Why the fuck did you have to kill them, you fucking cunt?' I screeched. 'They did nothing wrong to you!'

His confident manner remained unchanged as he put the tumbler back on the table. He appeared to consider my words for a moment, nodding slightly in reflection with his hands clasped and continuing to sit nonchalantly cross-legged. The music sounded delicately in the background, as if to add to the frustratingly contemptuous energy of the room. His calmness enraged me and he knew it; he was well aware that I wanted him to beg and squirm and suffer but was not willing to give me the satisfaction.

'No, you're right. They didn't do anything wrong,' he replied superciliously. 'But you did. Look at my house. It's a piece of shit. You and George both bent me over. You both stole a lot of money and I don't take too kindly to people stealing from me, Jack. Anyway, you should be happy. Because if you didn't have anything to do with it, I took care of the other two for you.'

'Fuck you!' I screamed as I pulled the trigger.

Time seemed to slow as the bullet travelled through the air to hit him in the left thigh. The world went quiet. Smoke billowed from the chamber of the gun in the dim lamplight. I didn't falter. My furious countenance held as I watched him.

His calm face had changed to convey a subtle shock. His eyes widened and he looked down to see the wound spurting with crimson. He dabbed at it with his hand and then moved it up to his face to survey the blood with a look of mild disbelief. He had the look of a man who had thought that I hadn't had the fortitude to actually pull the trigger, the look of a man who had thought that the verbal dance would have gone back and forth until I eventually lost my resolve.

'Jesus, Jack!' He groaned in discomfort. 'Look at what you've done, you bastard!'

I walked over to him with the gun at my side. I wanted to stare him in the face and have him meet the full force of my violent rage. I wanted him to struggle, and suffer, and hurt. Just like I had done. I wanted him to die slowly. And painfully. And wish that he was dead before he actually was. Just as I had.

I now stood a metre from him and beheld the man in front of me with repugnance. His pretentious hair was slicked back neatly and his evil face was cleanly shaven. His lip quivered slightly with the pain. Although, his face now predominantly displayed no emotion in an attempt to hide his struggle. His expression was obscured by a gangster bravado that refused to show his internal state of panic, even though he really wasn't used to things not going the way that he had planned.

My anger was ill-deterred in the slightest. This was the man who had taken everything from me that I had ever lived for. I felt nothing for him except hatred. His subdued figure wriggled in its chair to sit in a more upright position, moaning faintly in acknowledgment of his veiled agony. Our eyes met for a split second. In a swift action, he grabbed the decanter of scotch that was on his side table and leapt from his chair to swing it at my head. It took me completely by surprise.

It struck my head violently. I stumbled backwards and then plummeted to the ground, dropping the gun that I was holding. The decanter broke apart on impact with my head, leaving a jagged half for him to hold in his hand as he crashed to the floor.

He rested for a moment on all fours, unable to stand properly due to the gunshot wound to his leg. His face had changed from unemotional to malevolent and bloodthirsty. His black eyes glistened. With a foreboding look on his face, he crawled slowly over to me with his freshly acquired weapon. One arm moved ominously in front of the other as I groggily tried to comprehend the situation. I was stunned for the moment, frozen in bewilderment. Blood streamed from the side of my face. I was a frail deer in front of homicidal headlights.

Before I could react, Rocco drove the sharp glass shard deep into my abdomen. A caustic white-hot pain struck me as I yelped in agony, waking from my trance. I moved my legs to kick him with an abrupt blow to his chest, which shoved him a slight distance away from me. He fell backwards and dropped the glass shard that he held in his hand.

I grabbed the gun that lay close to me on the floor and let out an almighty scream as I pulled the trigger again. This explosion I heard – I was human now, not bulletproof or impenetrable. The bullet exploded from the chamber and landed in Rocco's stomach, accompanied by a wail of anguish from him. The evil was human. He was not a stony killer at that very moment, but rather vulnerable and under the threat of eradication.

He writhed in pain, clutching the wound to his midsection that began to gush blood and stain his robe. My ears wrung from the jarring sound of the gunshot. I touched my excruciating stab wound with one hand; it was deep and the blood that ran from it was warm on my palm. I felt slightly woozy, my energy weakened for the moment. I dazedly glared over at my nemesis. He was feeble and labouredly respiring. I strained with every ounce of strength that I had left within me to begin crawling over to him. The small distance between us felt like hundreds of metres. I agonisingly placed one arm in front of the other to reach him. My stomach burned along with my pounding head. I grunted loudly in pain with every movement. A deep cerise blood streamed from both of my wounds.

Rocco stared back at me helplessly, grasping his stomach with a fearfully petrified look painted on his face. I grabbed his foot and pulled myself closer to his prone body. He shrieked when my other hand was placed on the thigh that contained his initial bullet wound. I edged closer up his body. His fists swung in a weak attempt to fight me off but I was undeterred, my steely resolve had returned, making my strength unmatchable.

I pulled myself up until my eyes were level with the black eyes of my wife and daughter's killer. I could stare directly into them and gaze into his nefarious soul. He knew the end was nigh. His eyes were wide with fear. He respirated with a shallow rapidity. I had his life in my clutches. I had the power to take it away, just as he had done with Helena and Matilda's. His weakly desperate blows bounced off my head and body to no avail as he struggled under my body weight. I moved my hands to his throat and clasped it tightly, continuing to stare directly into his eyes that screamed back at me.

He clutched my wrists in a frantic attempt to deter me, groaning with desperate effort. His breathing choked and spluttered. I was unmoved. My power was monumental. I squeezed harder, tears running from my eyes as the thought of my perfectly innocent wife and daughter flashed through my mind. I couldn't feel any other sensations anymore, just the grip of my hands around his warm throat. It strained as it gasped for air, desperately attempting to fill the debilitated body that lay beneath me. I let out a howl that came from the depths of my soul with one last effort.

My arms bulged, engorged with dilated veins. I squeezed with all my might and pushed my body weight into his throat, his eyes shrieking in fearful pain. He was feeling only a glimpse of what I had felt ever since he had taken them away from me. But I wanted him to feel every second of it, right until his very end. I watched the life leave his eyes, feeling a complete flaccidity of his whole body. His pupils dilated and the gurgling stopped. I stayed there for a moment, frozen in my position and unable to release, staring at his lifeless eyes. I began to sob, mostly with relief at the fact that the ordeal was over, before falling back from the corpse onto the floor. I felt no sympathy for him. And hoped that he had suffered. Actually, I knew that he had. He had wished for instant death but it had come slowly and painfully, just like my grief had been received. It was then that the white-hot flash of pain gripped me once again. I clutched my stomach in immense agony, feeling the warmth of the wound that was bleeding heavily and staining my clothes in crimson blood. My head throbbed as I moved my forearm to wipe the substantial amount of claret that surged from the forehead cut. I painfully struggled to my feet, surveying the dead man that lay away from me on the ground. Despite the intense distress my body had succumbed to, a smile painted my lips. I felt a sense of complete vindication.

'Good riddance, you fucking dog,' I murmured as I limped away, a peaceful symphony reverberating from the record player in the background.

X.

A love that walks with me to the end of my days,

and gently wipes the tears that stream down my face.

It says, 'my darling, it appears our time has come to its end,

but please never fret nor fear, I will find you again.

For you, my dear, are my soul, my everlasting light,

our love would bloom in the darkest of winter time.

Our love is true and one that is evergreen,

it does not need a mouth to speak, or eyes in which to see.'

Chapter 26
I Will Follow You into the Dark

I got to the outside of Rocco's house via the front door and staggered my way onto the murky street. It was here that I looked up at the stars that shimmered in the sky with the half-crescent moon that shone down over me. My pain broke for an instant and I smiled back. Helena had always maintained that if we were apart, we could always look up at the night sky and instantly feel closer to each other, knowing that the other had looked up at that identical night sky and done the same at one point.

I closed my eyes; she was always with me. They both were. I made my way to the car and groaned as I carefully lowered myself in, closing the creaky door and starting off into the night. I drove wanderingly, growing lighter and foggier, my condition waning by the minute. An intensely sporadic pain gripped me as it pleased. I pondered on what to do in terms of my welfare in a languorous stupor. I was fading quickly; the blow to my abdomen had seemingly punctured something that my body deemed was important to its survival. I considered a trip to the hospital for employment of medical aid. Unfortunately, this option carried the risk of bringing with it the societal righteousness of the law, which would in turn contradict the justice that I had already delivered for myself. My only other option was to return to my antiquated fortress amongst the gum tree in Harvist Street, the home of love and everything in this world that I had held so dear. It proved quite the conundrum. The car's headlights navigated the quietly dark suburban streets as I wearily clutched the steering wheel and continued to deliberate on my next move.

I dipped in and out of consciousness, but somehow, I eventually found myself out the front of my home, seemingly guided by a subconscious autopilot that had known exactly where I needed to be. I didn't need a hospital – I needed my home; it was where I belonged. I left the car under the gum tree out the front and limped arduously towards the house. My heavy footsteps echoed loudly on the pavement and thudded on the veranda in the stillness of the street. My body, however, felt weightless, as if it was floating. I entered the pitch-black house, which was completely silent. The crack of the open door seemed to break its serenity. Blinds flapped lightly in the breeze through the broken windows at the back of the house as I rested for a moment in the open doorway. I stumbled down the corridor with my strenuously heavy gait banging on the floorboards and echoing against the nothingness. The bedroom door was flung open and I turned on the light, collapsing onto the soft bed and grimacing fiercely in the process. I turned to my side table and grabbed a picture of Helena, Matilda and myself that sat there, holding it up to look at it dotingly. The beaming faces all shone back at me in pure happiness. This picture was love. This picture was life. Most importantly, this was what was hopefully waiting for me at the termination of my imminently ending, perilous journey. I clutched the picture to my chest and held it tightly.

Epilogue

So, this is where I lay, on the bed, covered in the blood that runs from my wounds. My breathing grows increasingly difficult, my body heaves to intake oxygen. Life is fading from me, death approaches. I feel totally numb. *Am I a monster?* No, quite the contrary. I'm a man in love with the two most beautifully perfect beings that ever graced the earth. And I'm a man who was willing to do anything for the ones that I love. Because true love is rare, so if it is present, cherish it with every fibre of your being, in life and in death. Breathe and hang on through the strenuous times and be completely present and savour the pleasant times. Nourish and protect it in the tough moments and do not jump ship too readily when the stormy seas of life get rocky. Help the ship calm the storm and fight for the ones that you love, for it is the most powerful possession that you can have in this life. *What makes a seemingly normal man find the urge to kill?* Well, I would answer with this. *What makes men climb mountains? What makes men sail seas? What makes men go to war?* It's love. In one way or another, it is love. It's pursuit. It's protection. It's sustenance. A love of adventure, of ego, of one's country, of freedom, of a cause. Any other emotion would not simply justify such actions. Love is behind many of the things that we do, and also, many of the things that we never thought we were capable of doing.

There is no pain. I am no longer sad or angry. I am purely content.

'Here's to sweet revenge,' I whisper as I drift away to whatever the afterlife has to offer me.

I am at peace; I am finally free.

Shawline Publishing Group Pty Ltd
www.shawlinepublishing.com.au

SHAWLINE
PUBLISHING
GROUP

More great Shawline titles can be found by scanning the QR code below.
New titles also available through Books@Home Pty Ltd.
Subscribe today at www.booksathome.com.au or scan the QR code below.

Printed by BoD™in Norderstedt, Germany

More My Molar Pregnancy

Personal Stories From Diagnosis Through Recovery